TAO
The Little Samurai

#5

Wild Animals!

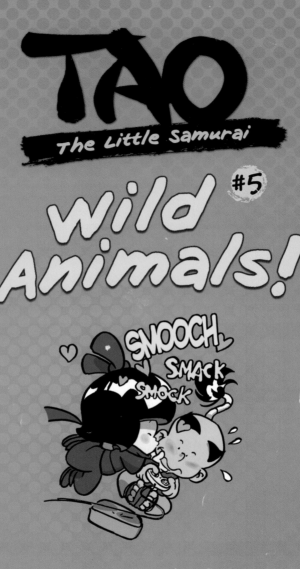

SMOOCH

SMACK

SMOCK

Laurent Richard
illustrated by Nicolas Ryser
Translation: Edward Gauvin

GRAPHIC UNIVERSE™ • MINNEAPOLIS

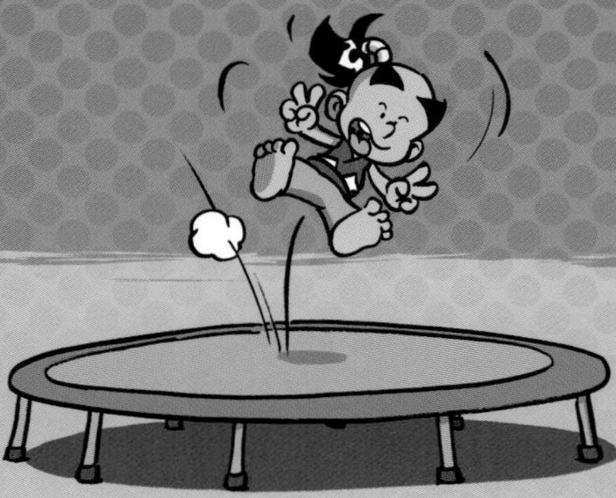

STORY BY LAURENT RICHARD
ILLUSTRATIONS BY NICOLAS RYSER
TRANSLATION BY EDWARD GAUVIN

FIRST AMERICAN EDITION PUBLISHED IN 2014 BY GRAPHIC UNIVERSE™.

NEM PAS MAL! BY LAURENT RICHARD AND NICOLAS RYSER © BAYARD ÉDITIONS, 2011
COPYRIGHT © 2014 BY LERNER PUBLISHING GROUP, INC., FOR THE US EDITION

GRAPHIC UNIVERSE™ IS A TRADEMARK OF LERNER PUBLISHING GROUP, INC.

GRAPHIC UNIVERSE™
A DIVISION OF LERNER PUBLISHING GROUP, INC.
241 FIRST AVENUE NORTH
MINNEAPOLIS, MN 55401 USA

FOR READING LEVELS AND MORE INFORMATION,
LOOK UP THIS TITLE AT WWW.LERNERBOOKS.COM.

MAIN BODY TEXT SET IN CCWILDWORDS 8.5/10.5.
TYPEFACE PROVIDED BY FONTOGRAPHER.

LIBRARY OF CONGRESS CATALOGING-IN-PUBLICATION DATA

RICHARD, LAURENT, 1968–
    [NEM PAS MAL! ENGLISH]
    WILD ANIMALS! / BY LAURENT RICHARD ; ILLUSTRATED BY NICOLAS RYSER ; TRANSLATION:
EDWARD GAUVIN. — FIRST AMERICAN EDITION.
        P.   CM. — (TAO, THE LITTLE SAMURAI ; #5)
    SUMMARY: TRAINING AT MASTER SNOW'S DOJO TAKES A TWIST WHEN NEW STUDENT RUBY
ARRIVES AND DISTRACTS SOME OF THE STUDENTS FROM THEIR PRACTICE, WHICH NOW INCLUDES
WORKING WITH ANIMALS.
    ISBN 978-1-4677-2098-4 (LIB. BDG. : ALK. PAPER)
    ISBN 978-1-4677-4662-5 (EBOOK)
    1. GRAPHIC NOVELS. [1. GRAPHIC NOVELS. 2. MARTIAL ARTS—FICTION. 3. SAMURAI—FICTION.
4. ZOO ANIMALS—FICTION.] I. RYSER, NICOLAS, ILLUSTRATOR. II. GAUVIN, EDWARD, TRANSLATOR.
III. TITLE.
PZ7.7.R5WIL 2014
741.5'944—DC23   2013038070

MANUFACTURED IN THE UNITED STATES OF AMERICA
1 – VI – 7/15/14

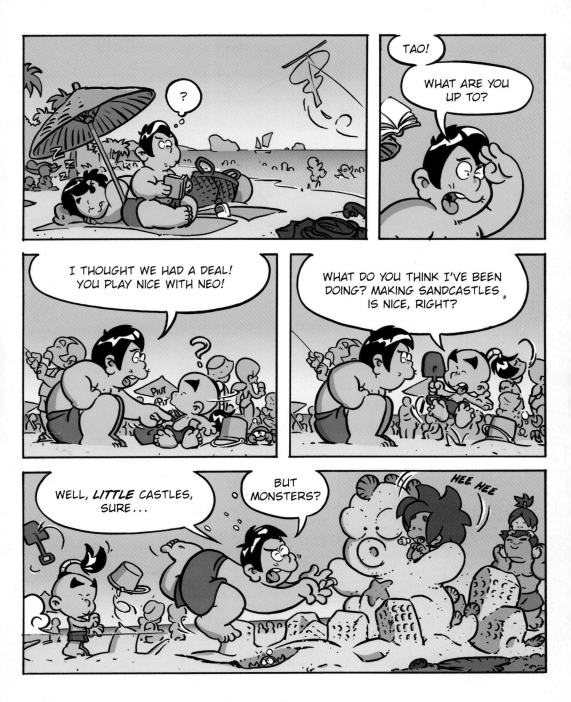

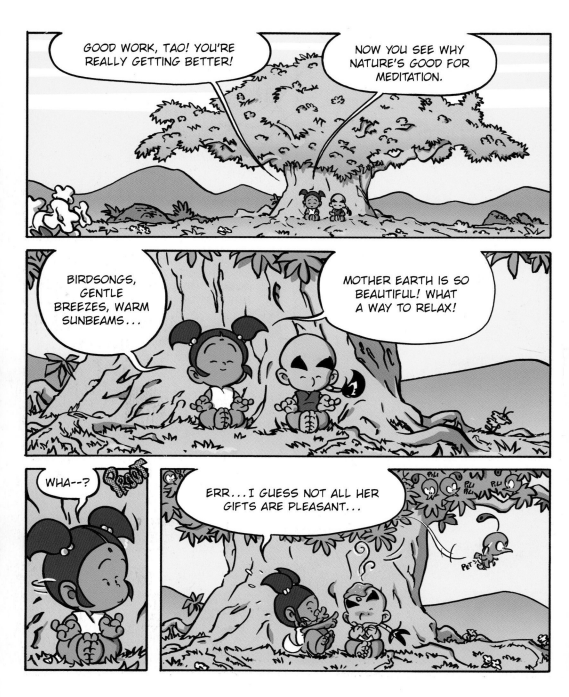

4

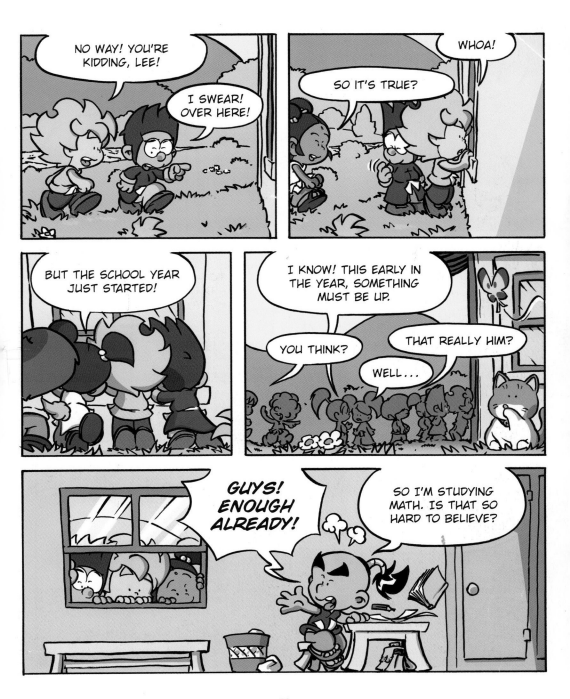

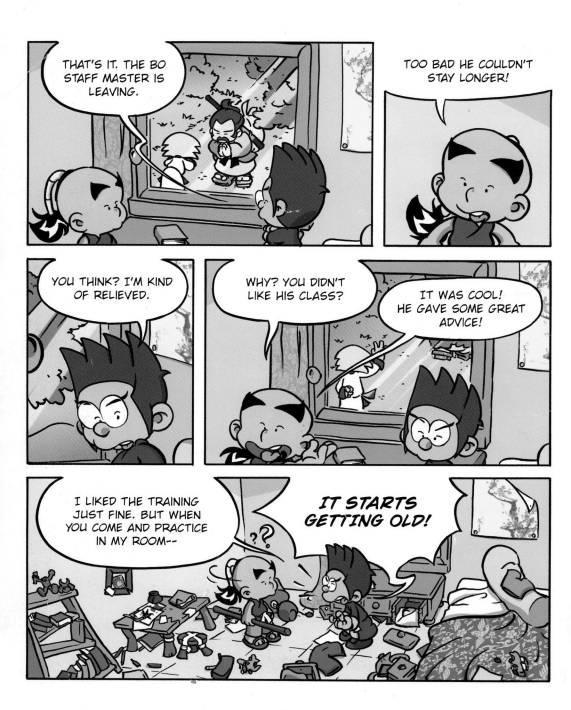

6

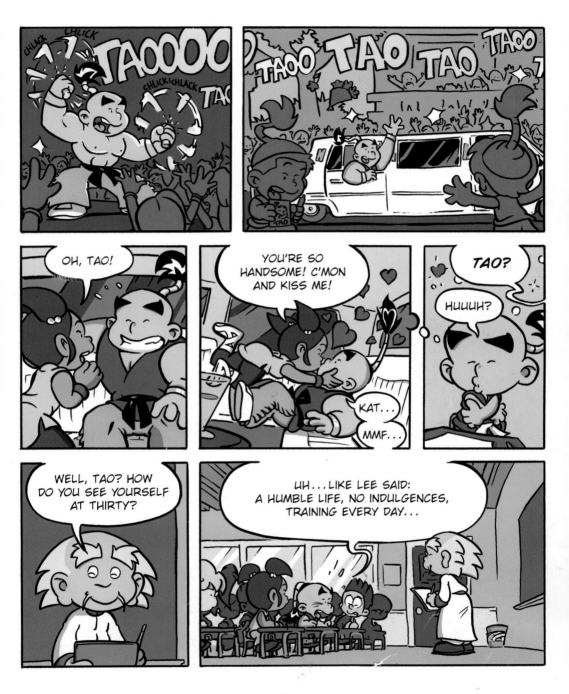

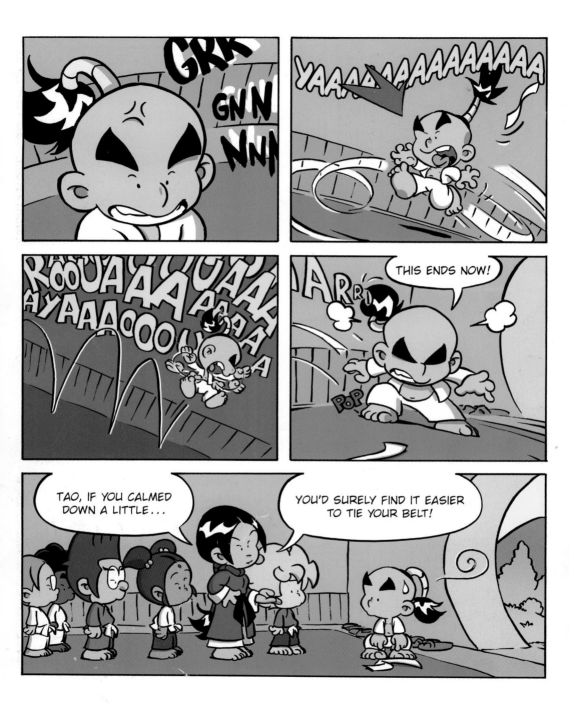

8

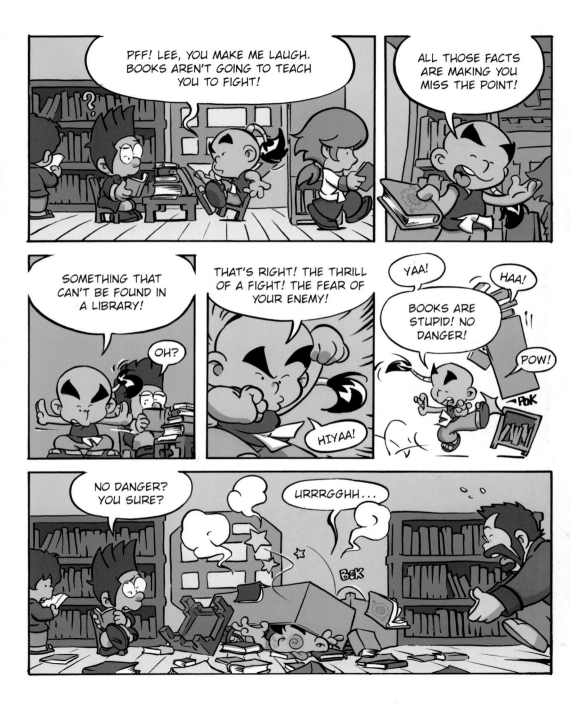

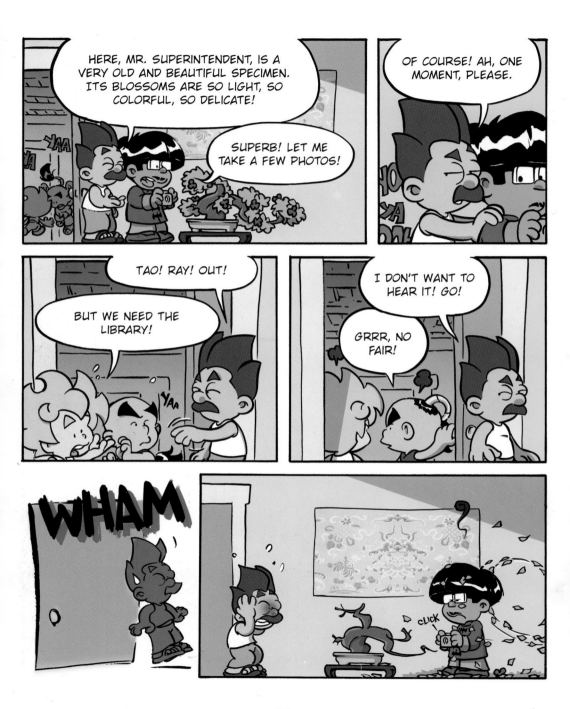

10

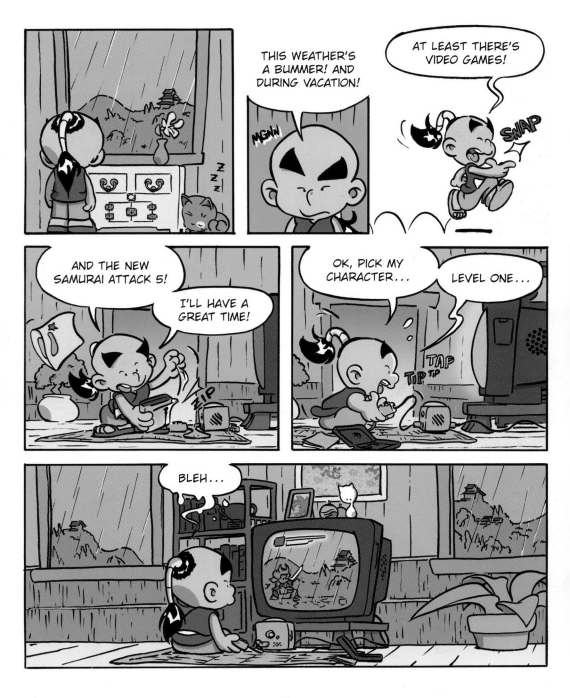

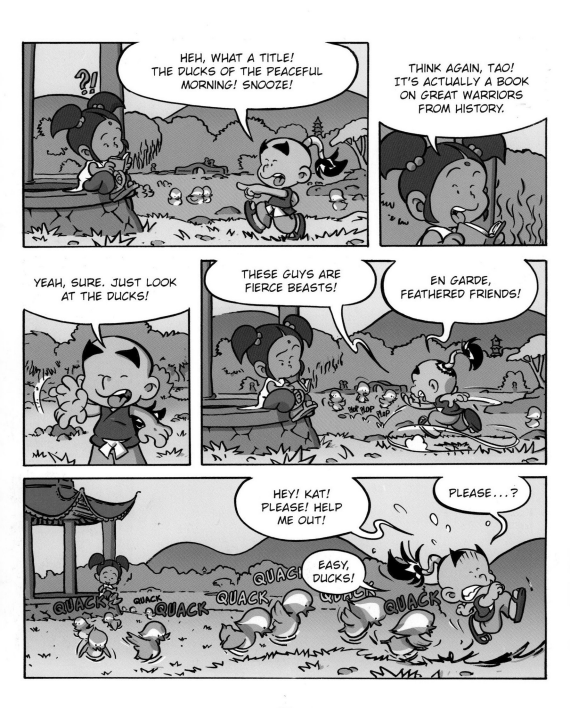

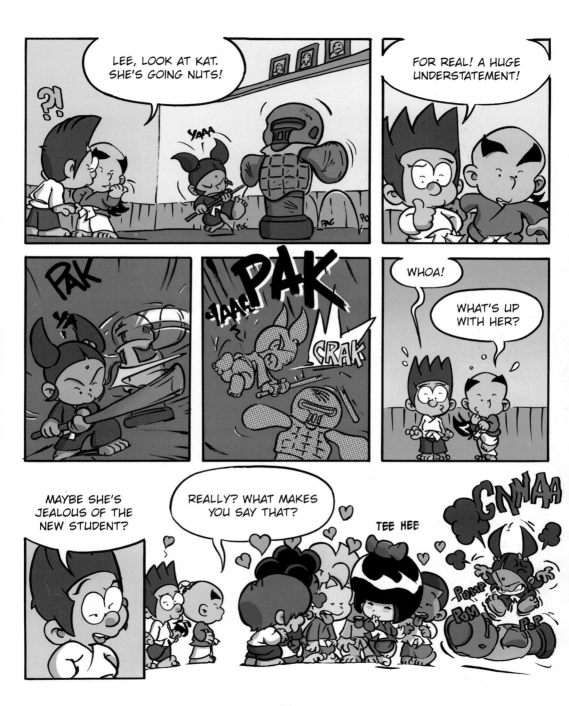

13

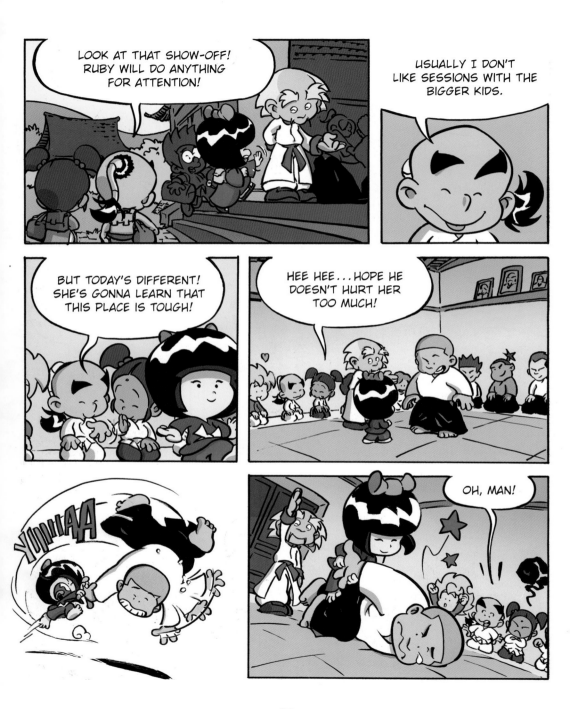

14

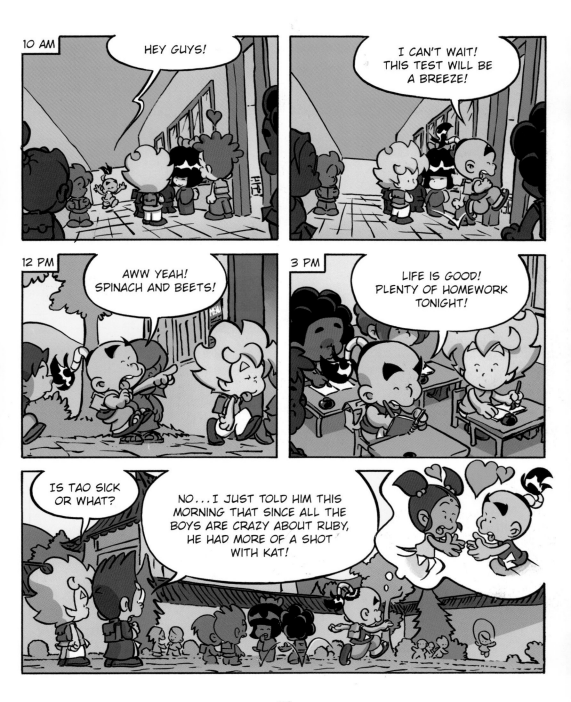

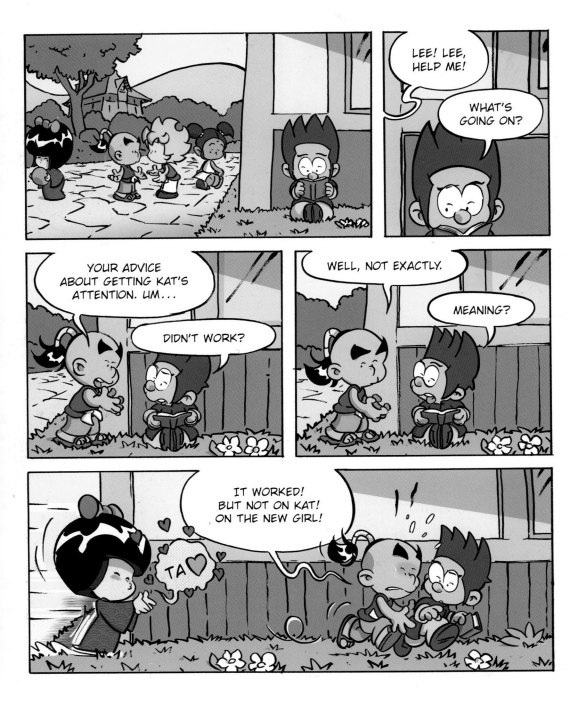

16

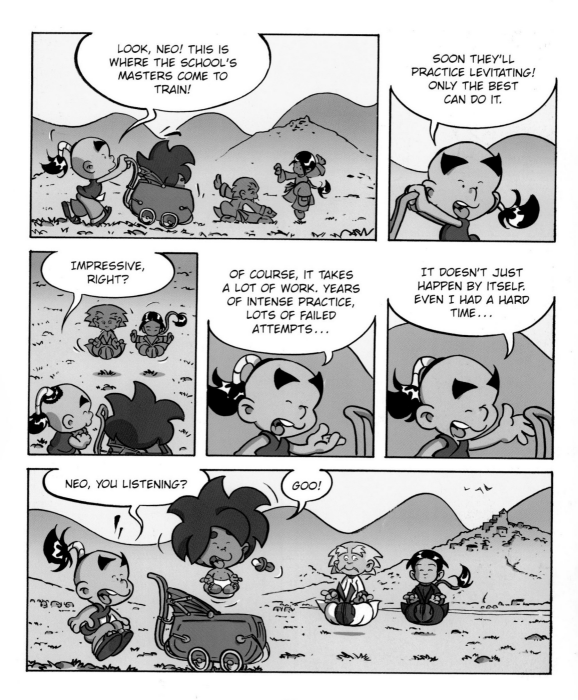

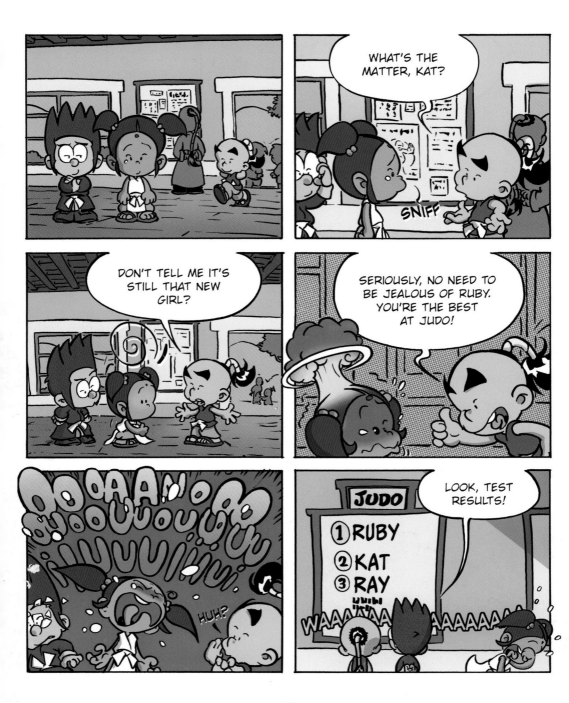

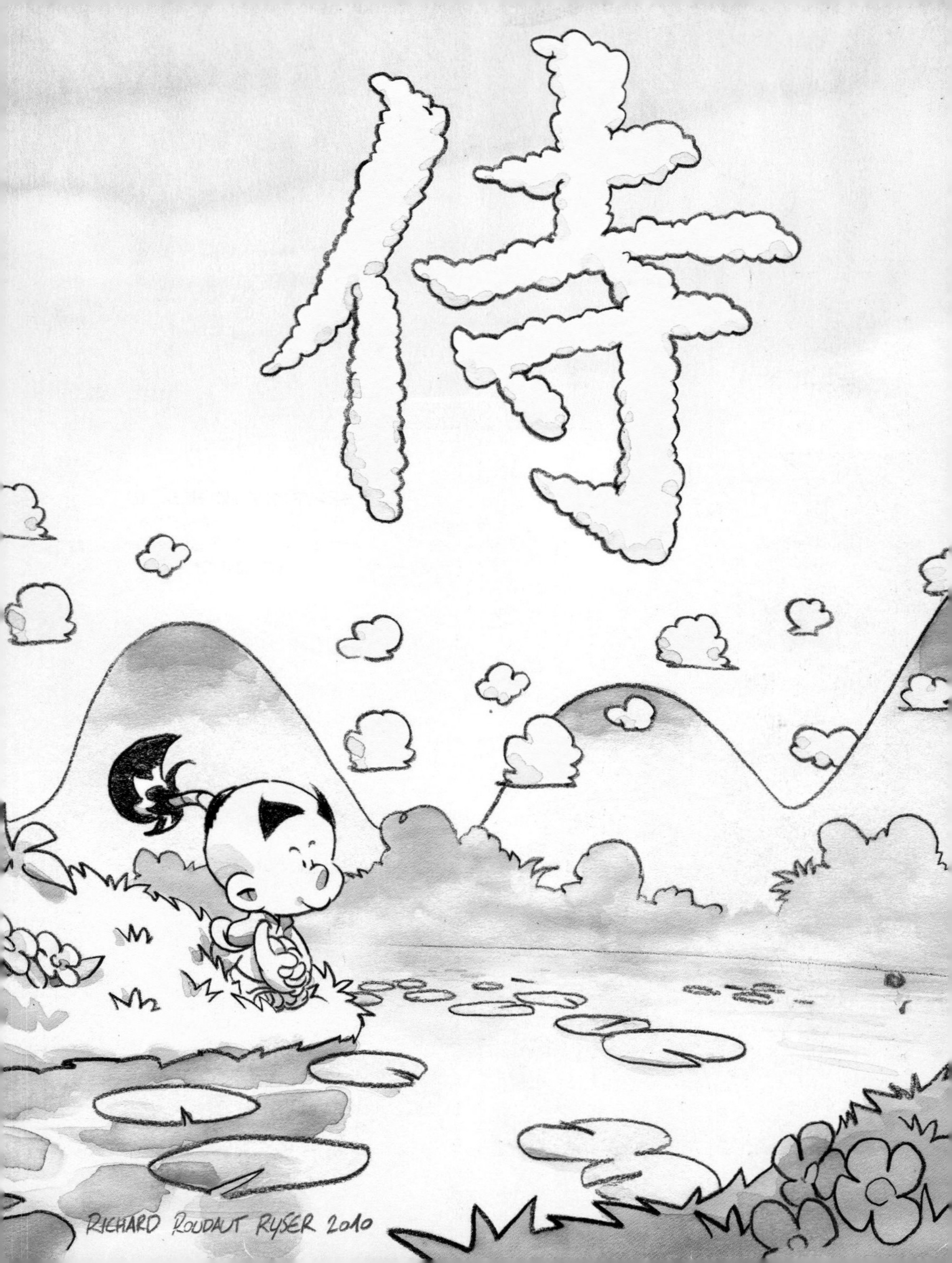
侍
RICHARD ROUDAUT RYSER 2010

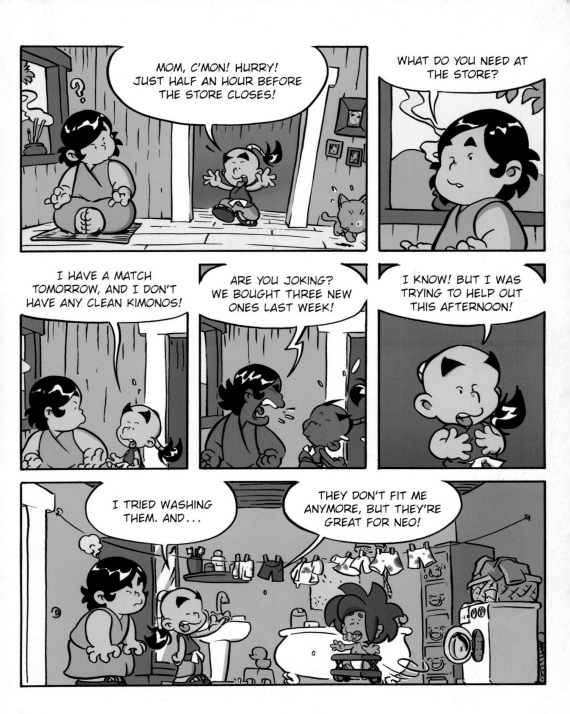

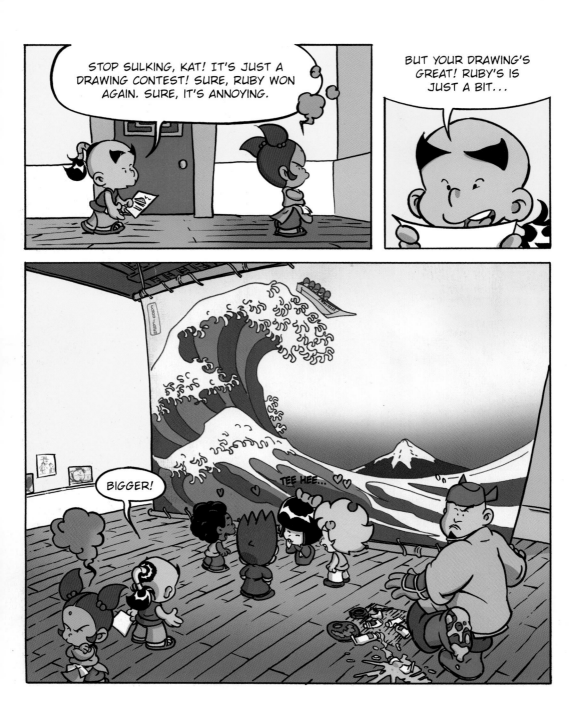

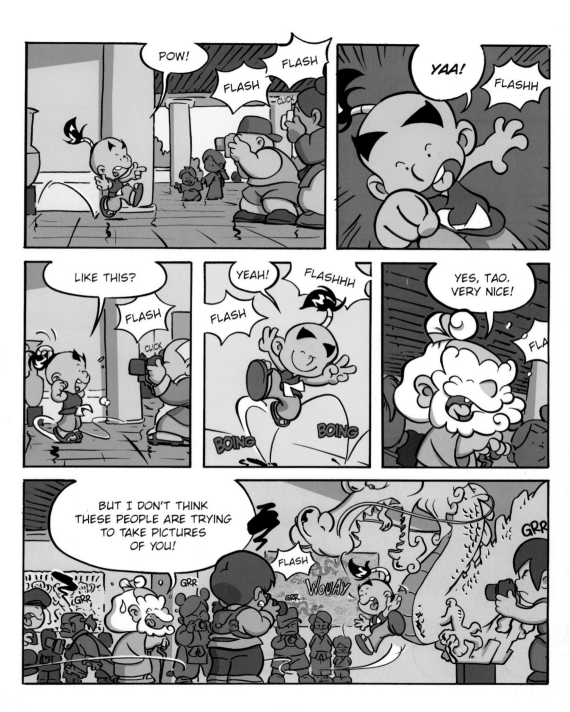

23

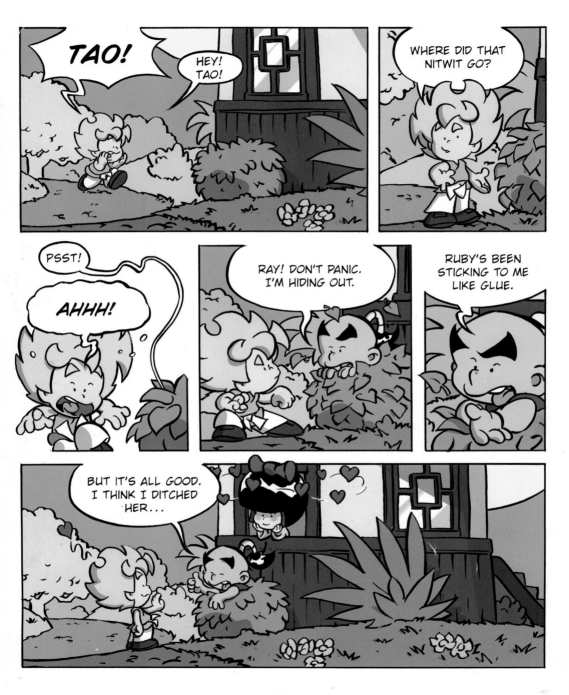

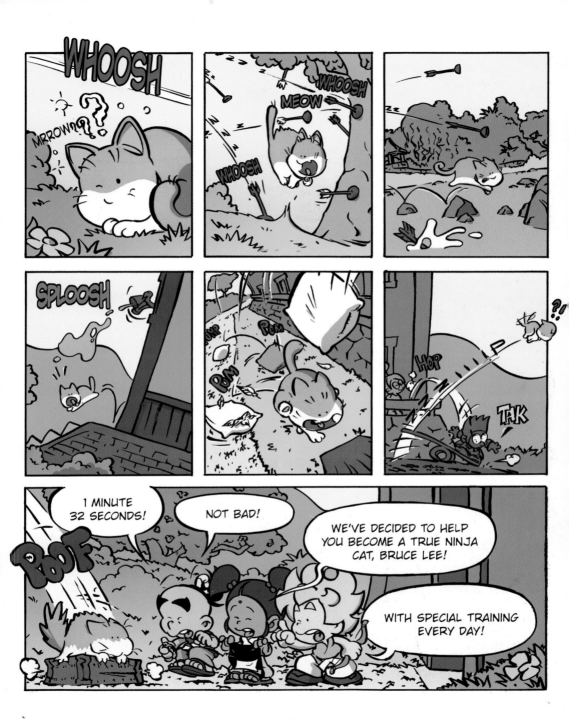

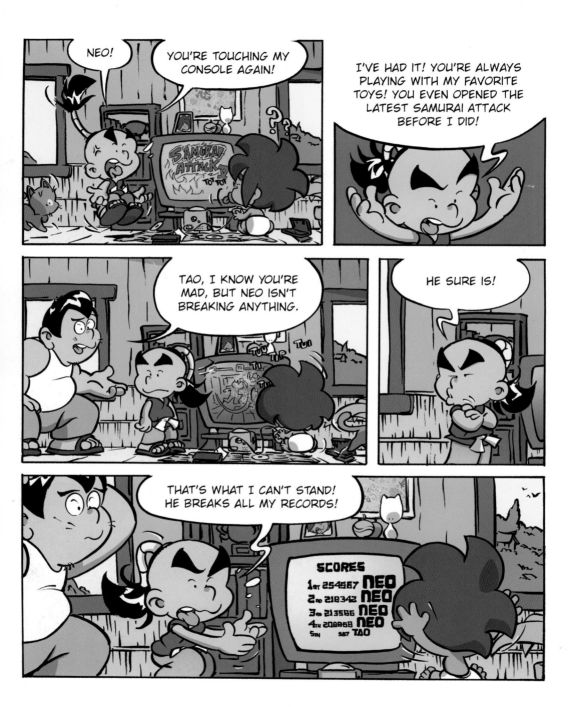

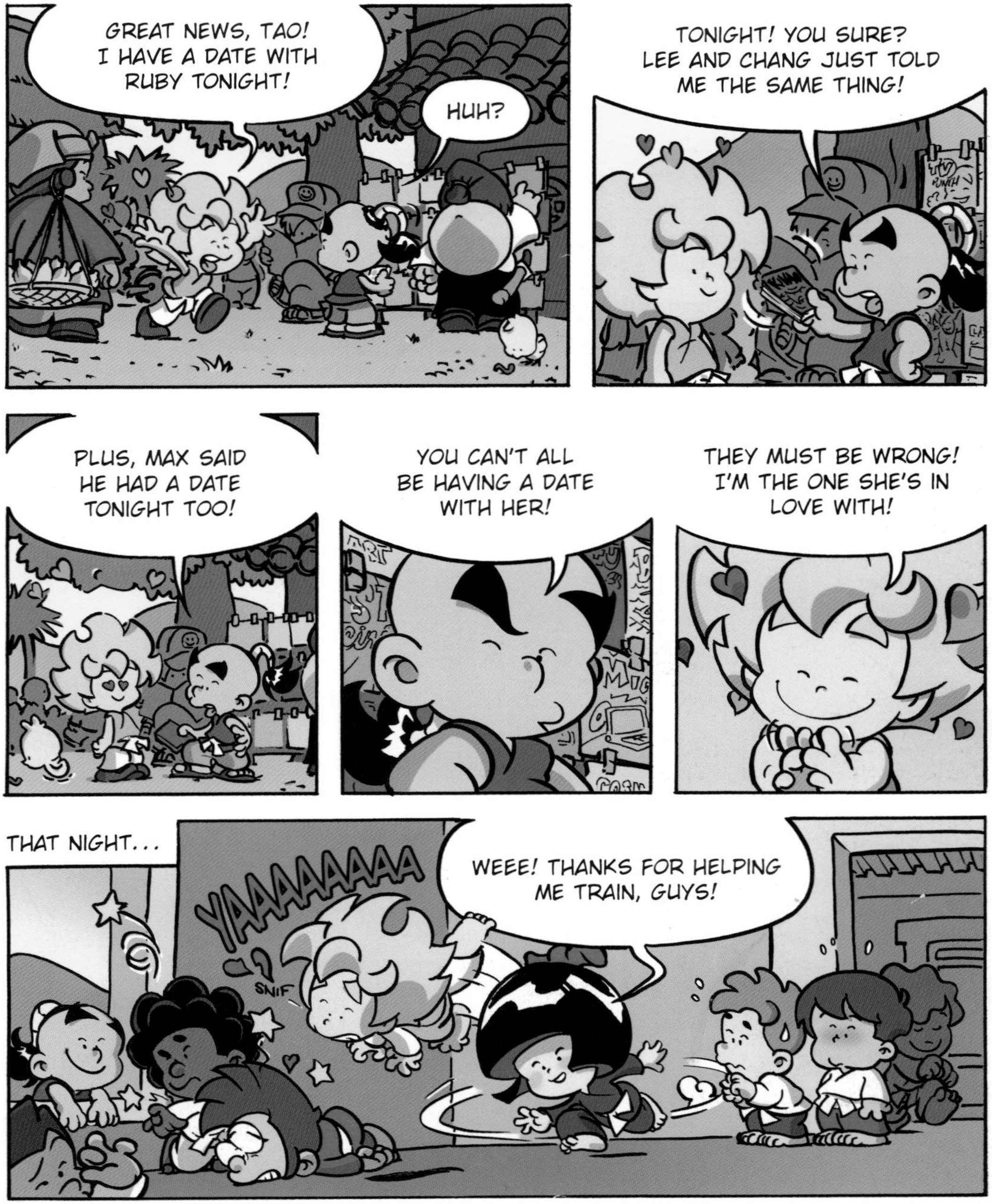
GREAT NEWS, TAO! I HAVE A DATE WITH RUBY TONIGHT!
HUH?
TONIGHT! YOU SURE? LEE AND CHANG JUST TOLD ME THE SAME THING!
PLUS, MAX SAID HE HAD A DATE TONIGHT TOO!
YOU CAN'T ALL BE HAVING A DATE WITH HER!
THEY MUST BE WRONG! I'M THE ONE SHE'S IN LOVE WITH!
THAT NIGHT...
YAAAAAAAA
SNIF
WEEE! THANKS FOR HELPING ME TRAIN, GUYS!

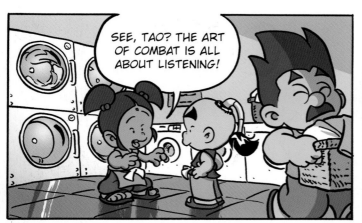

SEE, TAO? THE ART OF COMBAT IS ALL ABOUT LISTENING!

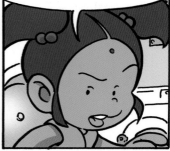

YOU HAVE TO BE ALERT TO THE SLIGHTEST SOUND!

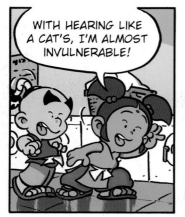

WITH HEARING LIKE A CAT'S, I'M ALMOST INVULNERABLE!

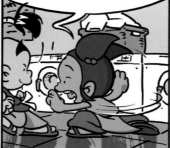

AT THE RUSTLE OF A BUTTERFLY'S WINGS, I'M READY!

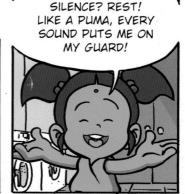

SILENCE? REST! LIKE A PUMA, EVERY SOUND PUTS ME ON MY GUARD!

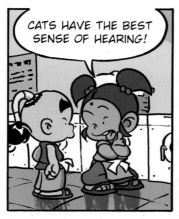

CATS HAVE THE BEST SENSE OF HEARING!

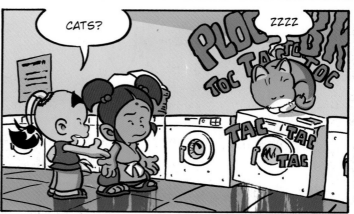

CATS?

PLOC TOC TAC TOC

ZZZZ

TAC TAC TAC

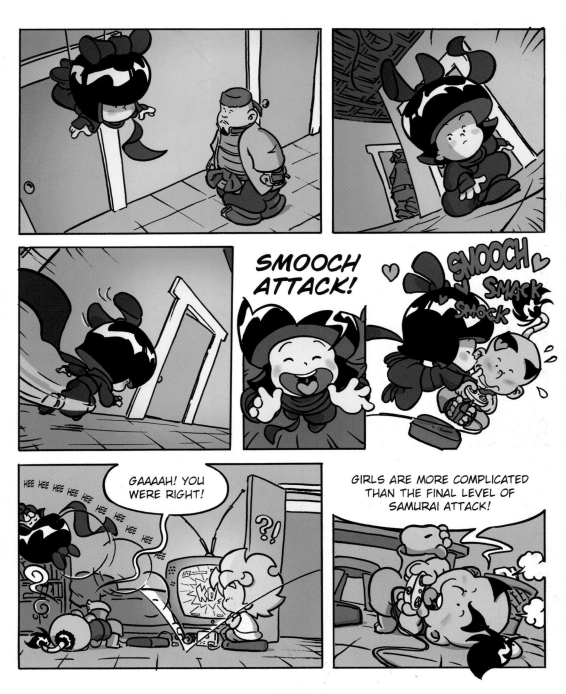

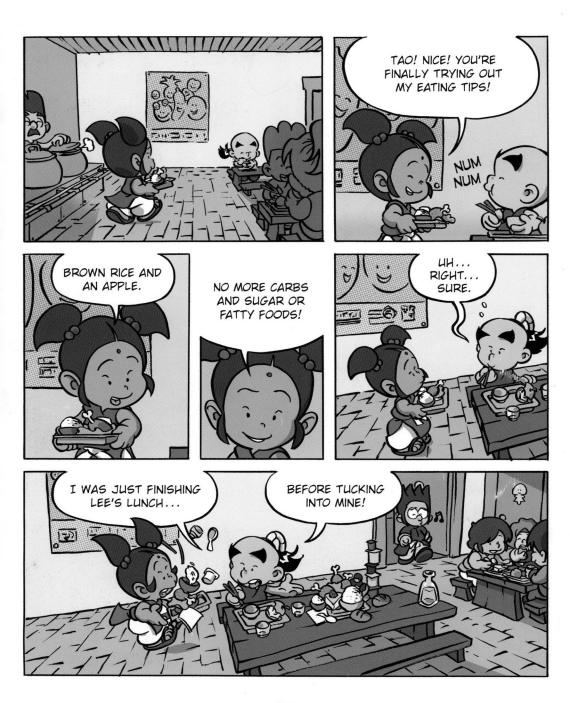

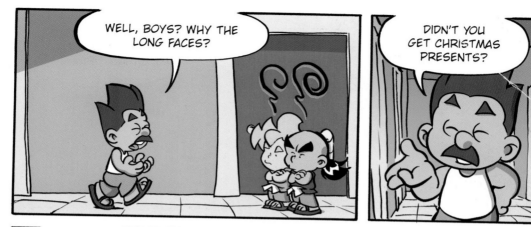

WELL, BOYS? WHY THE LONG FACES?

DIDN'T YOU GET CHRISTMAS PRESENTS?

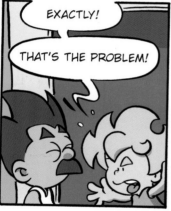

EXACTLY!

THAT'S THE PROBLEM!

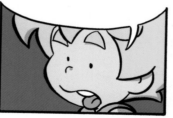

WE'RE STUDENTS AT A MARTIAL ARTS SCHOOL. FANS OF KARATE, KUNG FU, AND VIDEO GAMES!

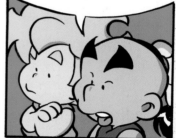

FANS OF MANGA, SAMURAI, ARMOR, AND ALL THAT STUFF!

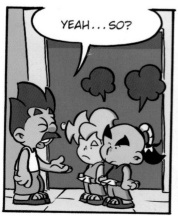

YEAH...SO?

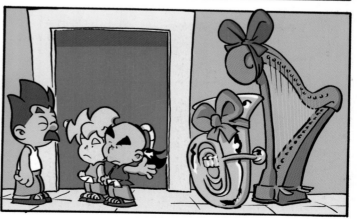

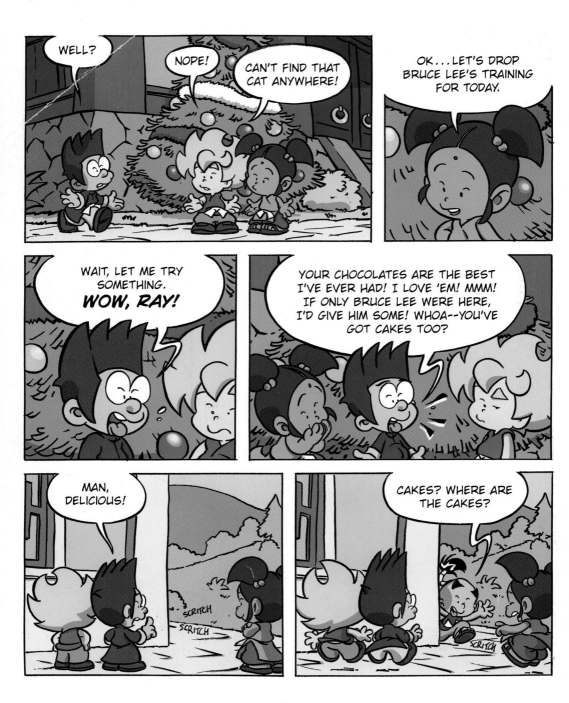

32

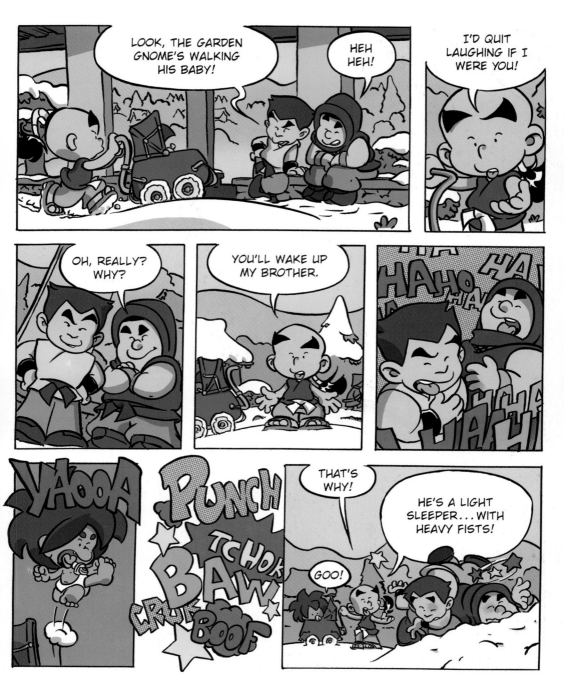

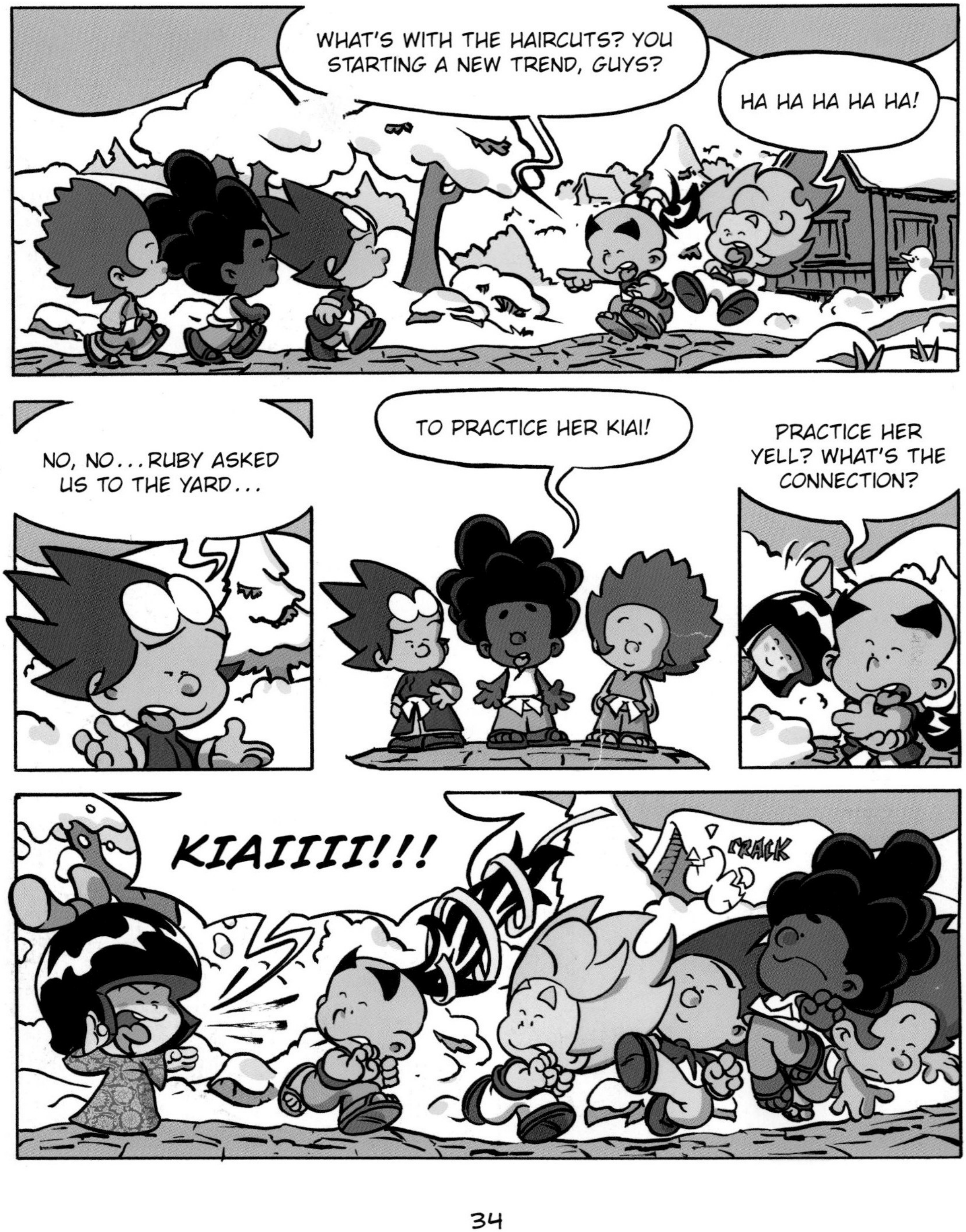
WHAT'S WITH THE HAIRCUTS? YOU STARTING A NEW TREND, GUYS?
HA HA HA HA HA!
NO, NO . . . RUBY ASKED US TO THE YARD . . .
TO PRACTICE HER KIAI!
PRACTICE HER YELL? WHAT'S THE CONNECTION?
KIAIIIII!!!
CRACK

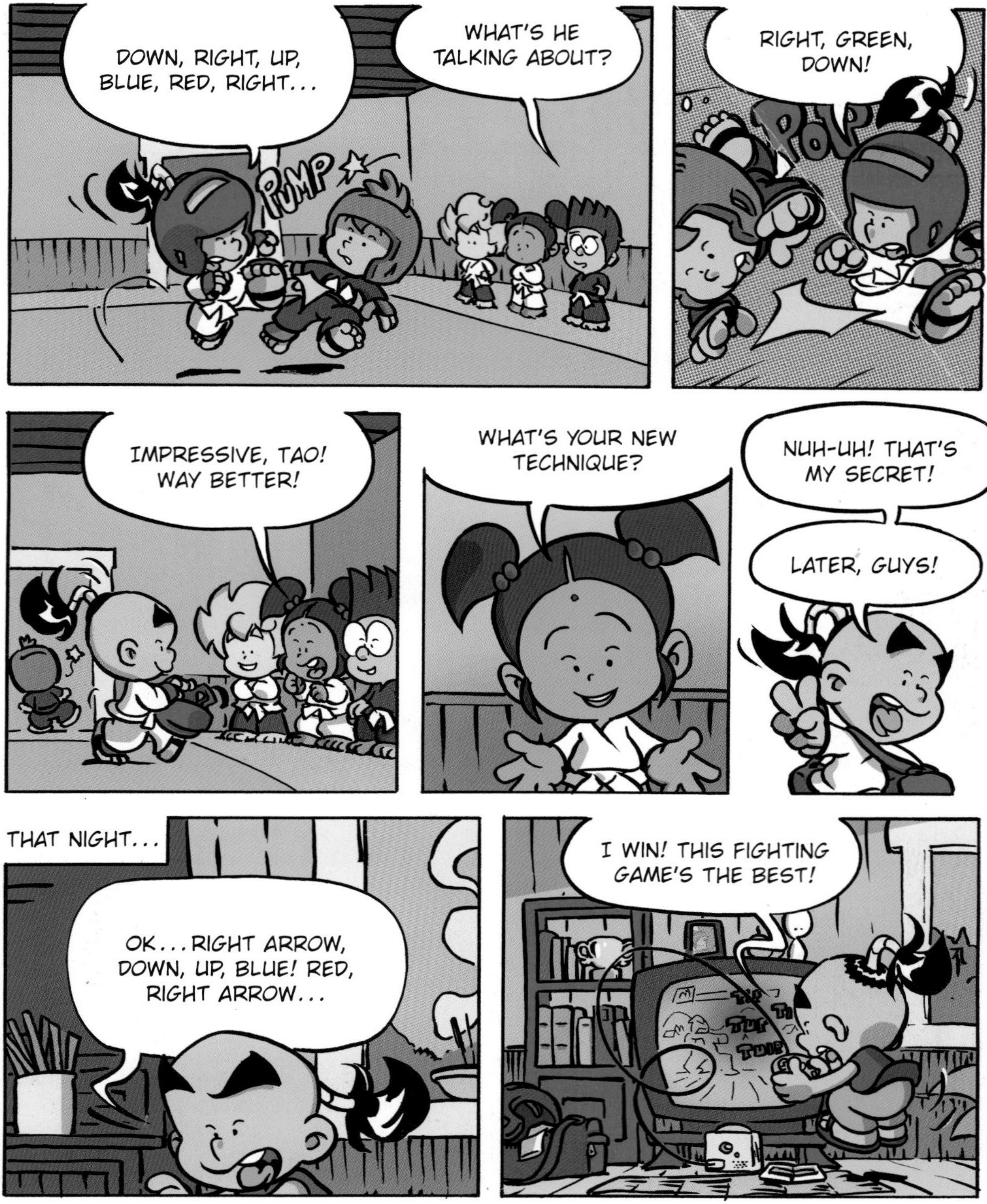
DOWN, RIGHT, UP, BLUE, RED, RIGHT...
WHAT'S HE TALKING ABOUT?
PUMP
RIGHT, GREEN, DOWN!
POP
IMPRESSIVE, TAO! WAY BETTER!
WHAT'S YOUR NEW TECHNIQUE?
NUH-UH! THAT'S MY SECRET!
LATER, GUYS!
THAT NIGHT...
OK... RIGHT ARROW, DOWN, UP, BLUE! RED, RIGHT ARROW...
I WIN! THIS FIGHTING GAME'S THE BEST!

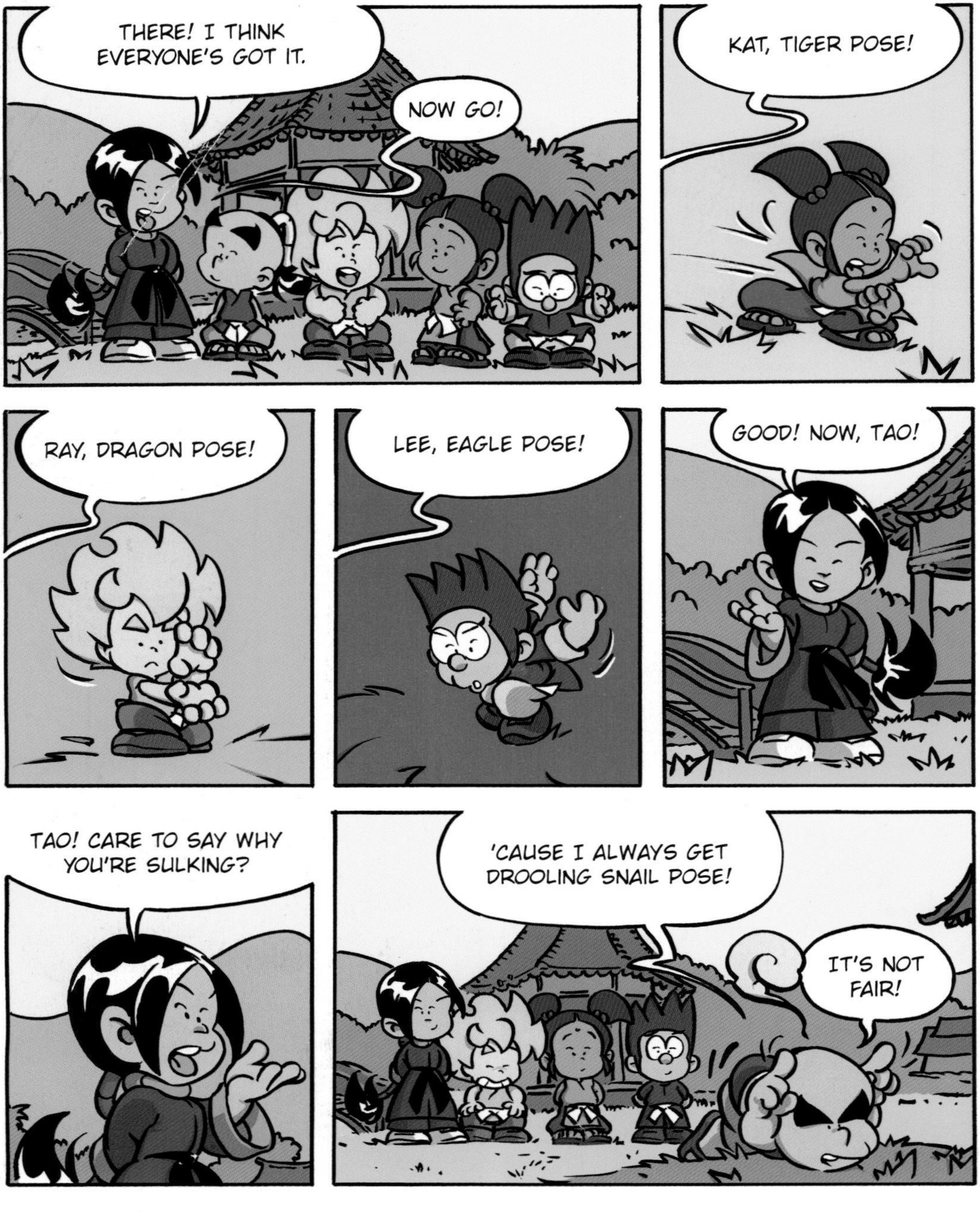
THERE! I THINK EVERYONE'S GOT IT.
NOW GO!
KAT, TIGER POSE!
RAY, DRAGON POSE!
LEE, EAGLE POSE!
GOOD! NOW, TAO!
TAO! CARE TO SAY WHY YOU'RE SULKING?
'CAUSE I ALWAYS GET DROOLING SNAIL POSE!
IT'S NOT FAIR!

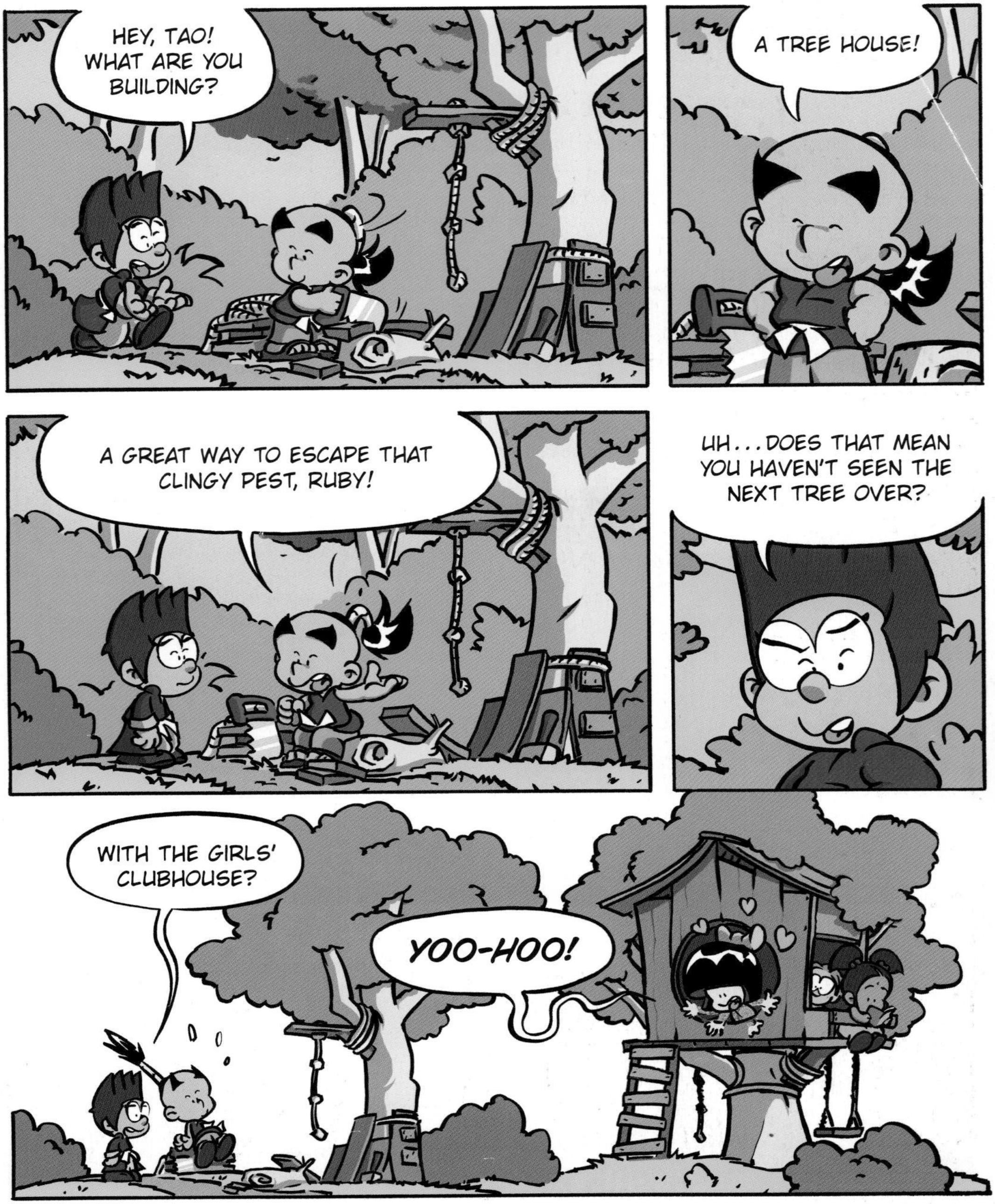
HEY, TAO! WHAT ARE YOU BUILDING?
A TREE HOUSE!
A GREAT WAY TO ESCAPE THAT CLINGY PEST, RUBY!
UH...DOES THAT MEAN YOU HAVEN'T SEEN THE NEXT TREE OVER?
WITH THE GIRLS' CLUBHOUSE?
YOO-HOO!

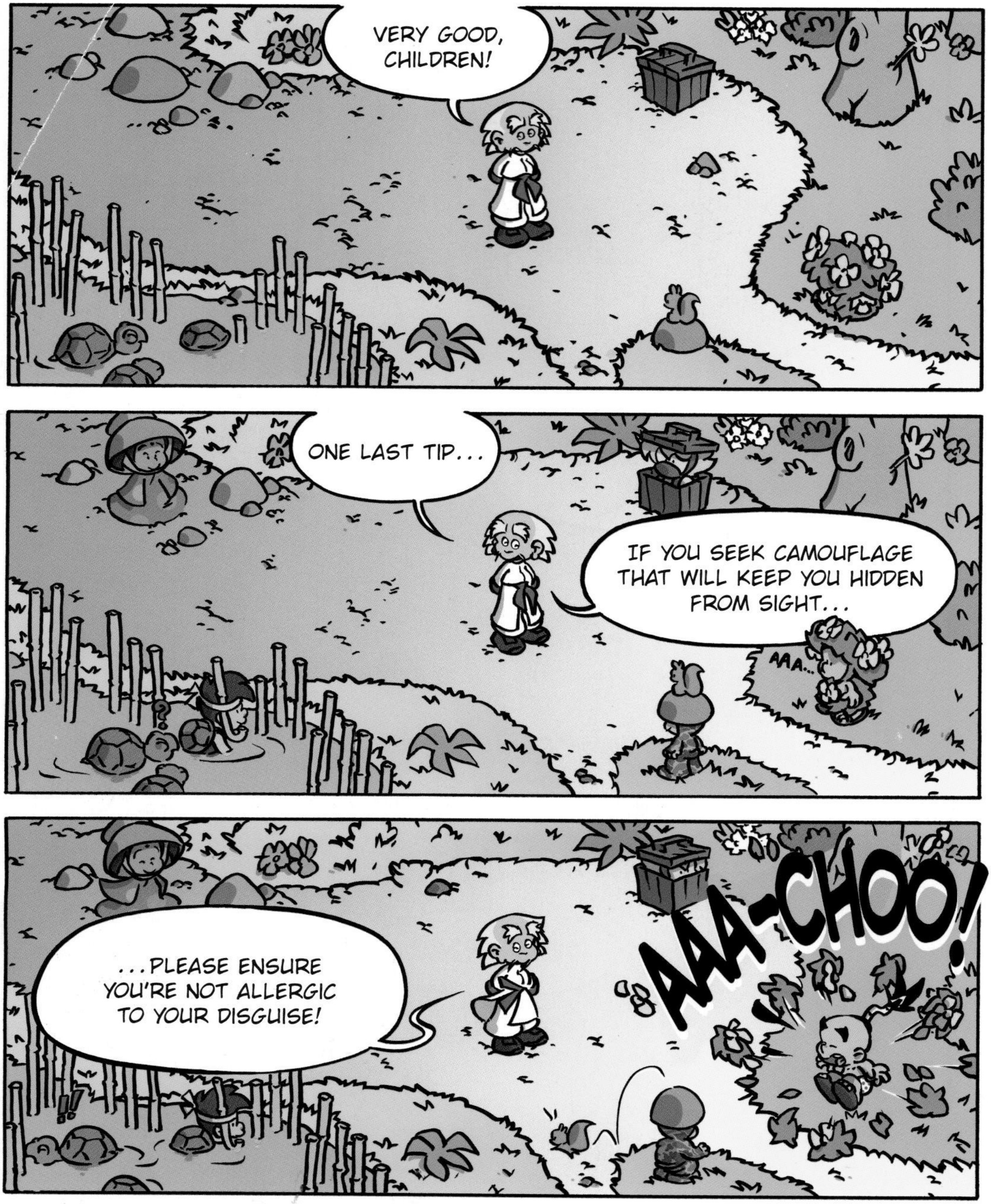
VERY GOOD, CHILDREN!
ONE LAST TIP...
IF YOU SEEK CAMOUFLAGE THAT WILL KEEP YOU HIDDEN FROM SIGHT...
AAA...
...PLEASE ENSURE YOU'RE NOT ALLERGIC TO YOUR DISGUISE!
AAA-CHOO!

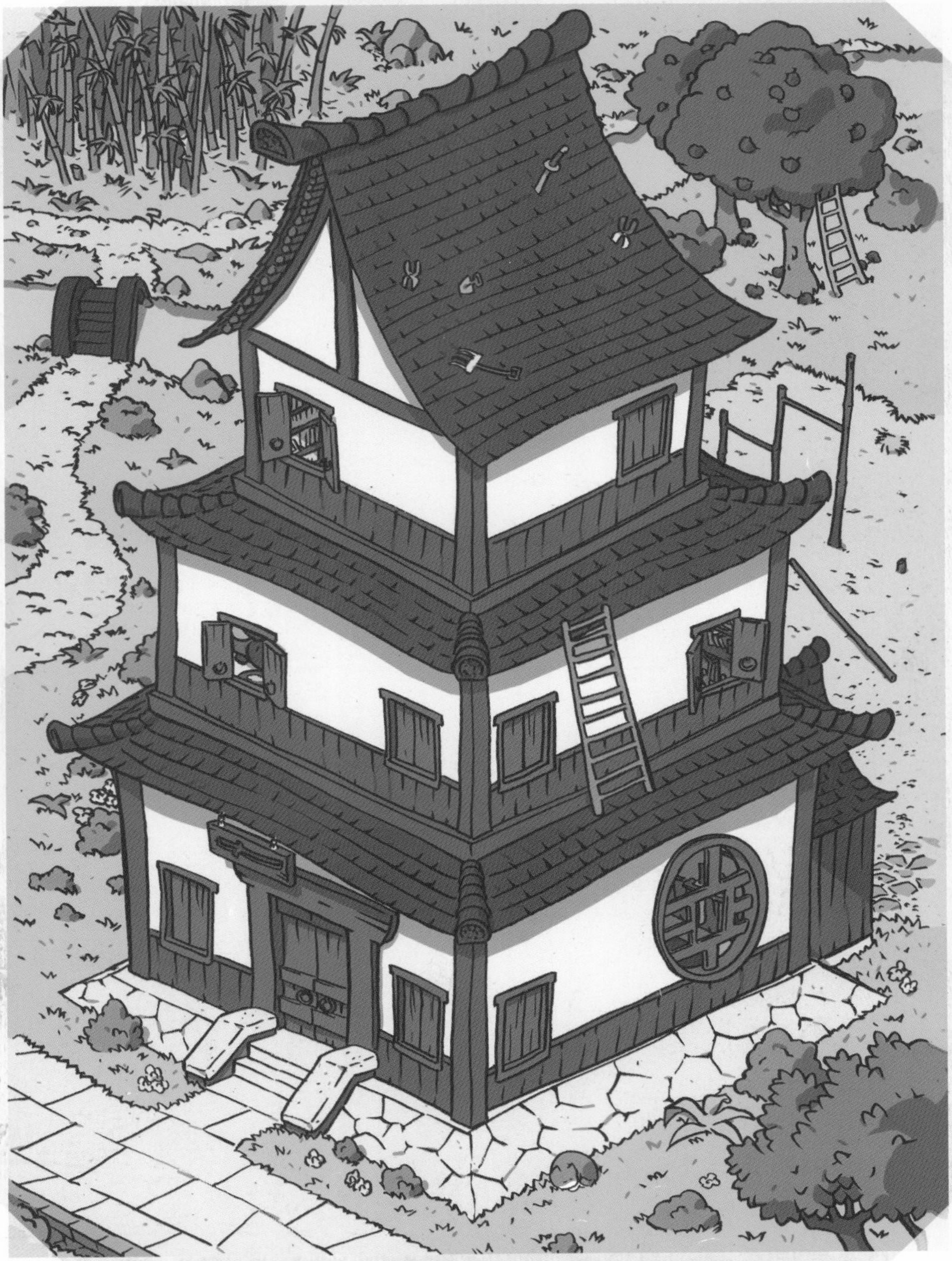

The Original Snow Academy

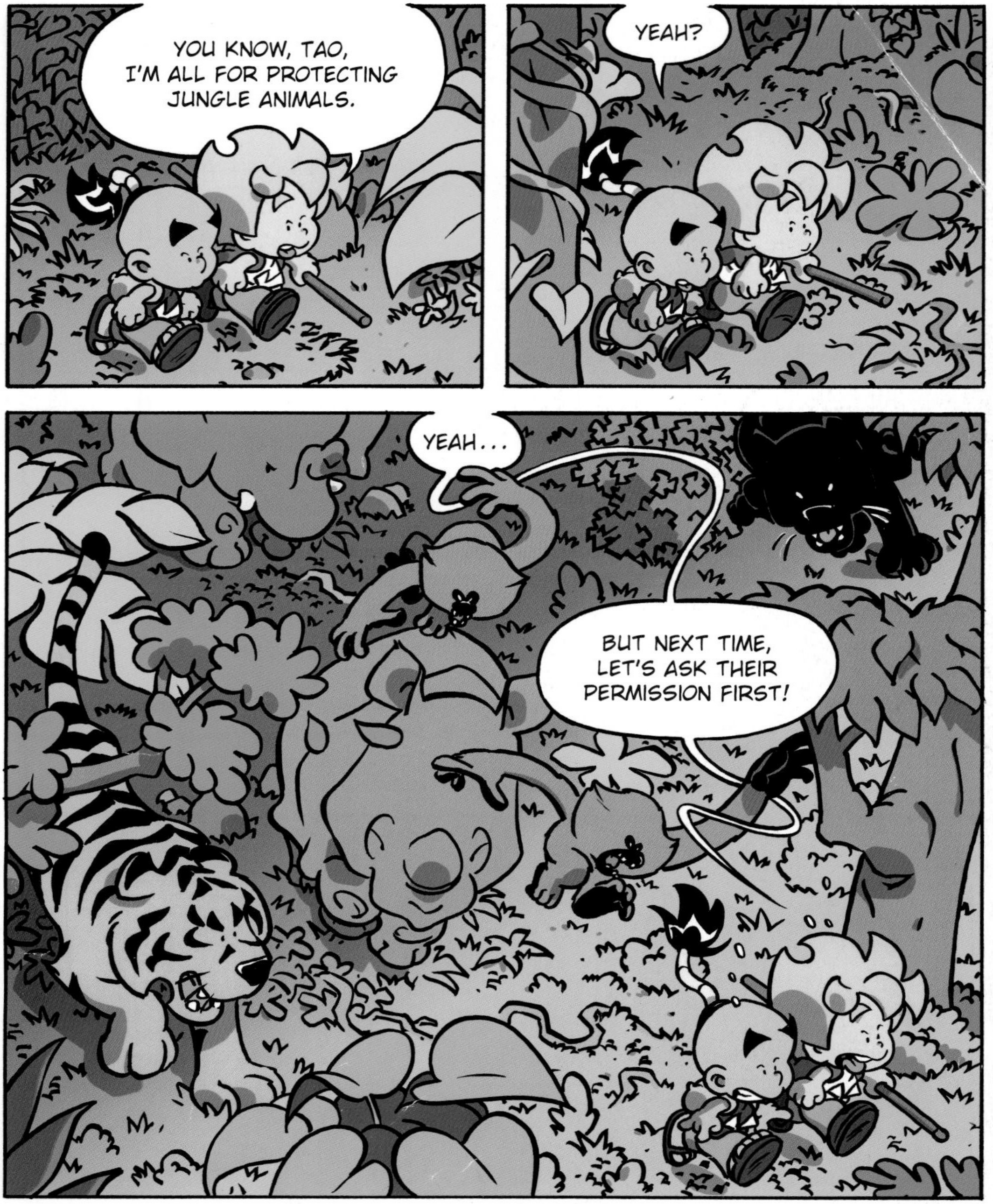
YOU KNOW, TAO, I'M ALL FOR PROTECTING JUNGLE ANIMALS.
YEAH?
YEAH...
BUT NEXT TIME, LET'S ASK THEIR PERMISSION FIRST!

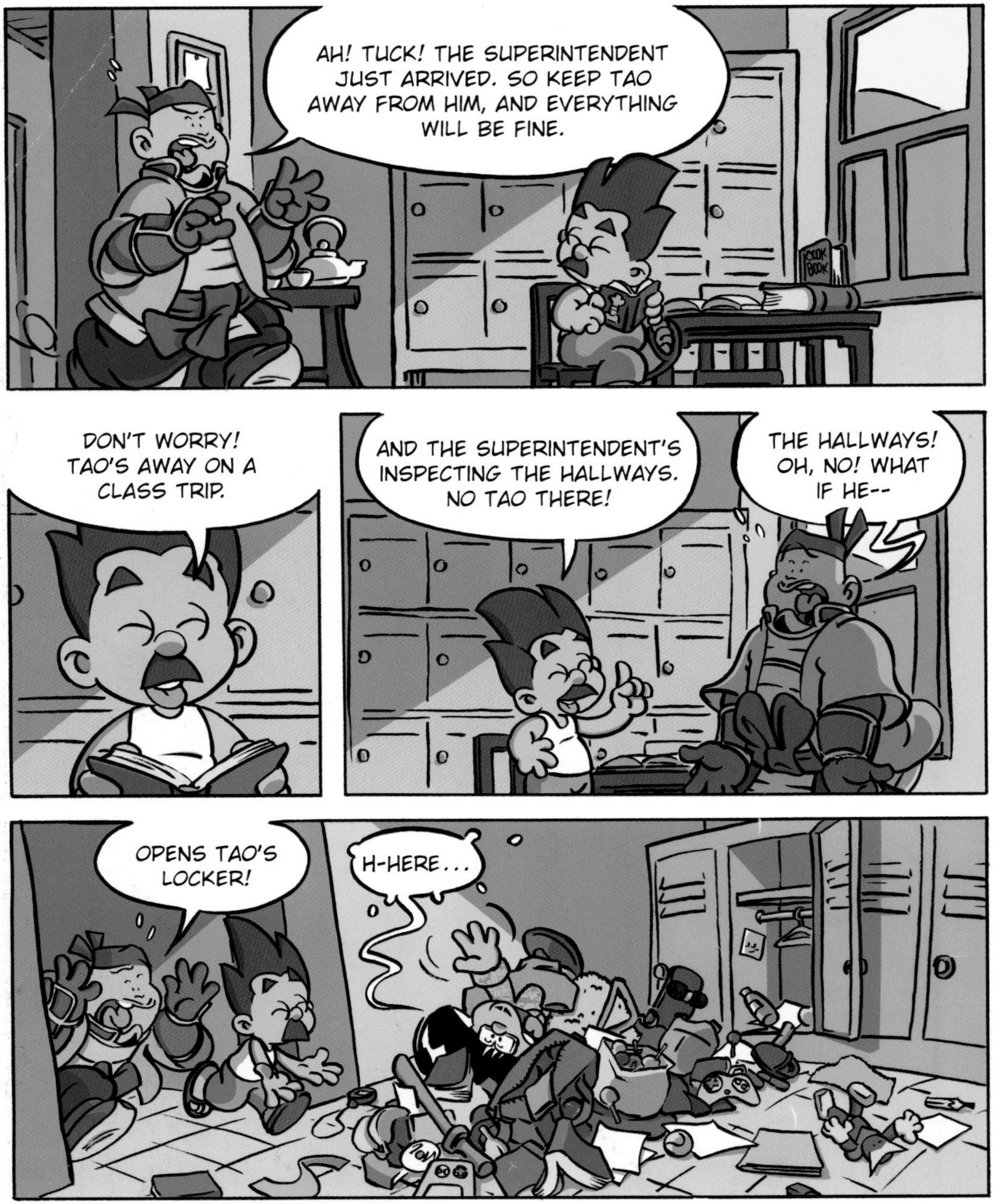
AH! TUCK! THE SUPERINTENDENT JUST ARRIVED. SO KEEP TAO AWAY FROM HIM, AND EVERYTHING WILL BE FINE.
COOK BOOK
DON'T WORRY! TAO'S AWAY ON A CLASS TRIP.
AND THE SUPERINTENDENT'S INSPECTING THE HALLWAYS. NO TAO THERE!
THE HALLWAYS! OH, NO! WHAT IF HE--
OPENS TAO'S LOCKER!
H-HERE . . .

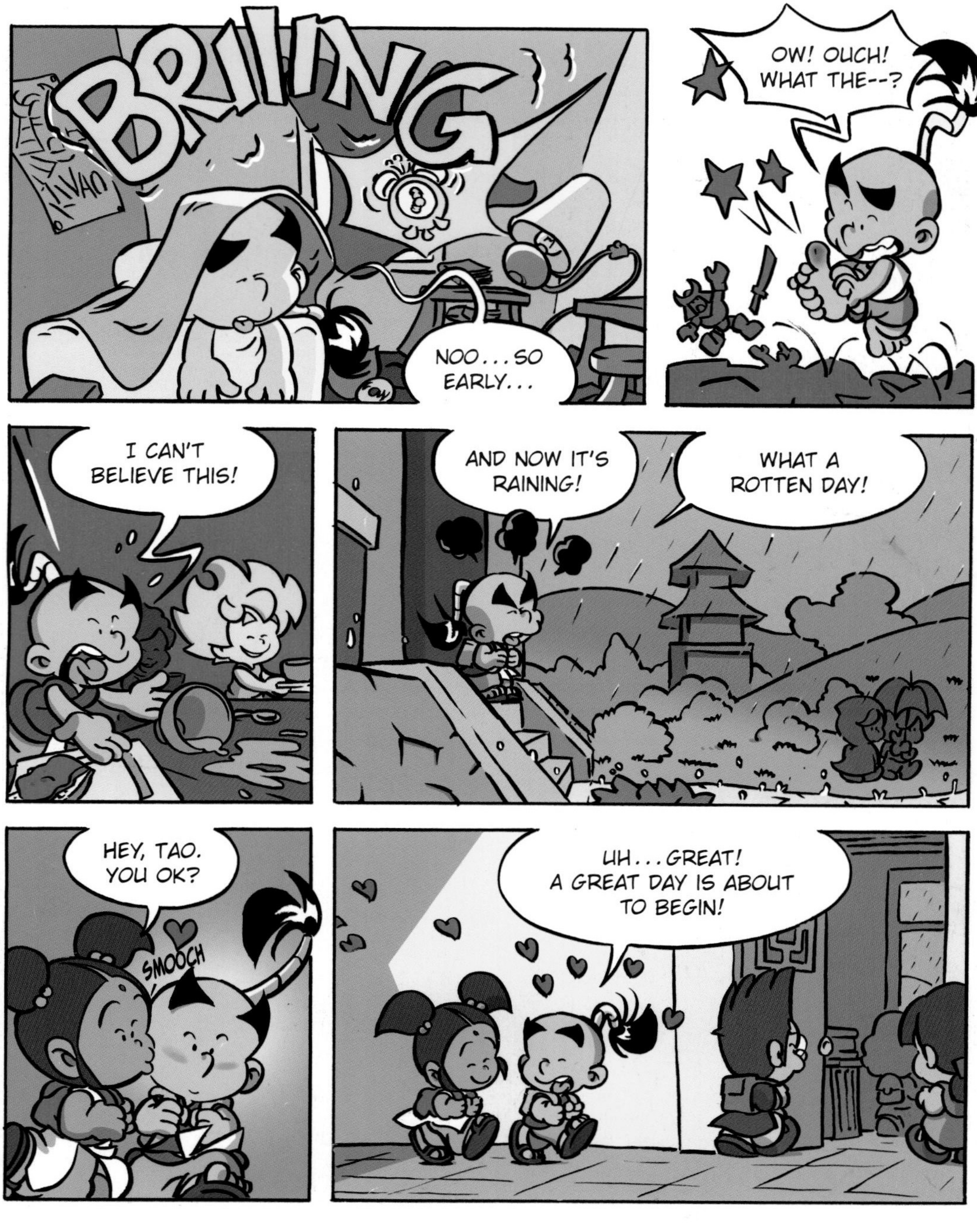
BRIIING
NOO...SO EARLY...
OW! OUCH! WHAT THE--?
I CAN'T BELIEVE THIS!
AND NOW IT'S RAINING!
WHAT A ROTTEN DAY!
HEY, TAO. YOU OK?
SMOOCH
UH...GREAT! A GREAT DAY IS ABOUT TO BEGIN!

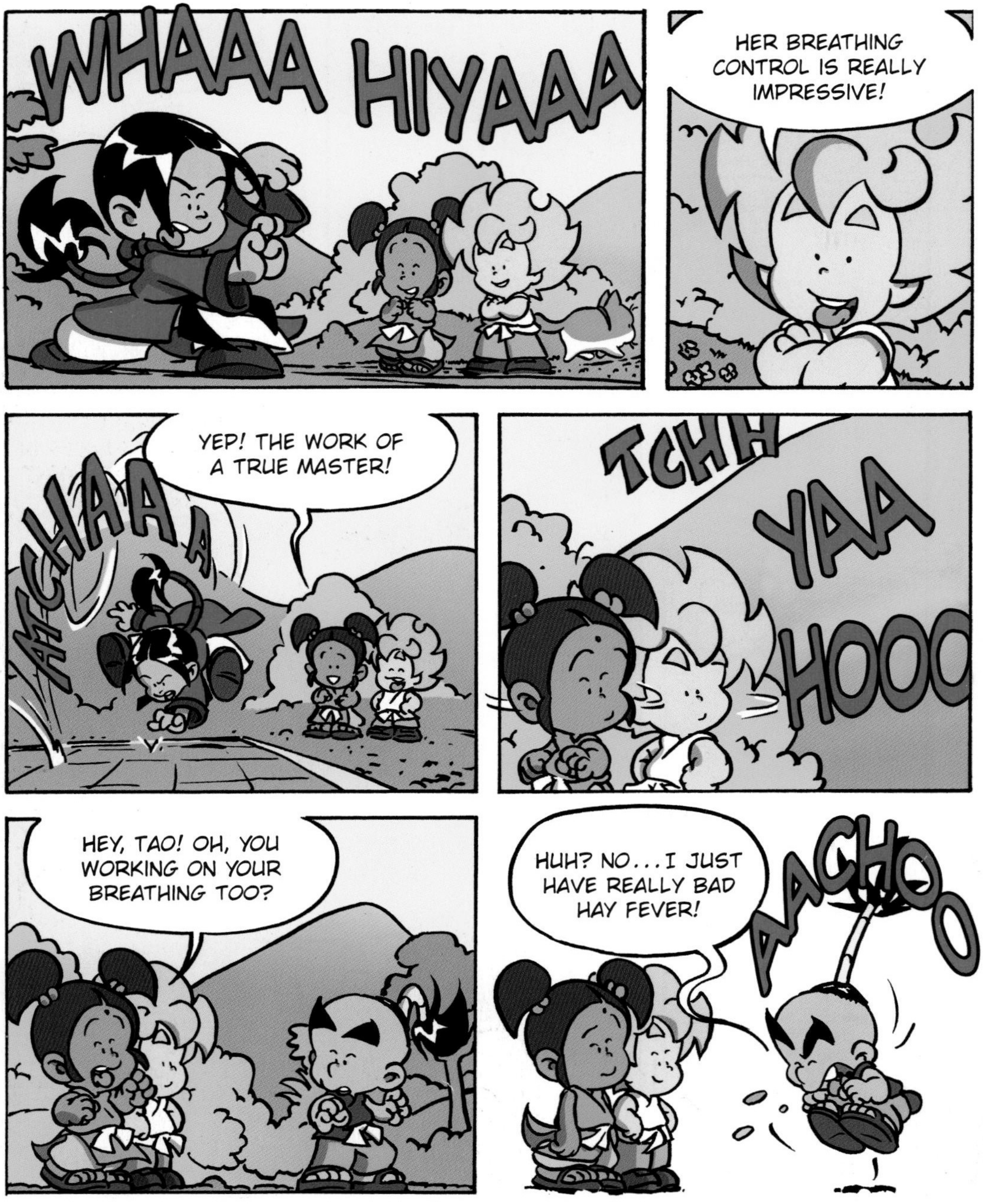
WHAAA HIYAAA
HER BREATHING CONTROL IS REALLY IMPRESSIVE!
ATCHAAAA
YEP! THE WORK OF A TRUE MASTER!
TCHH
YAA
HOOO
HEY, TAO! OH, YOU WORKING ON YOUR BREATHING TOO?
HUH? NO . . . I JUST HAVE REALLY BAD HAY FEVER!
AACHOO

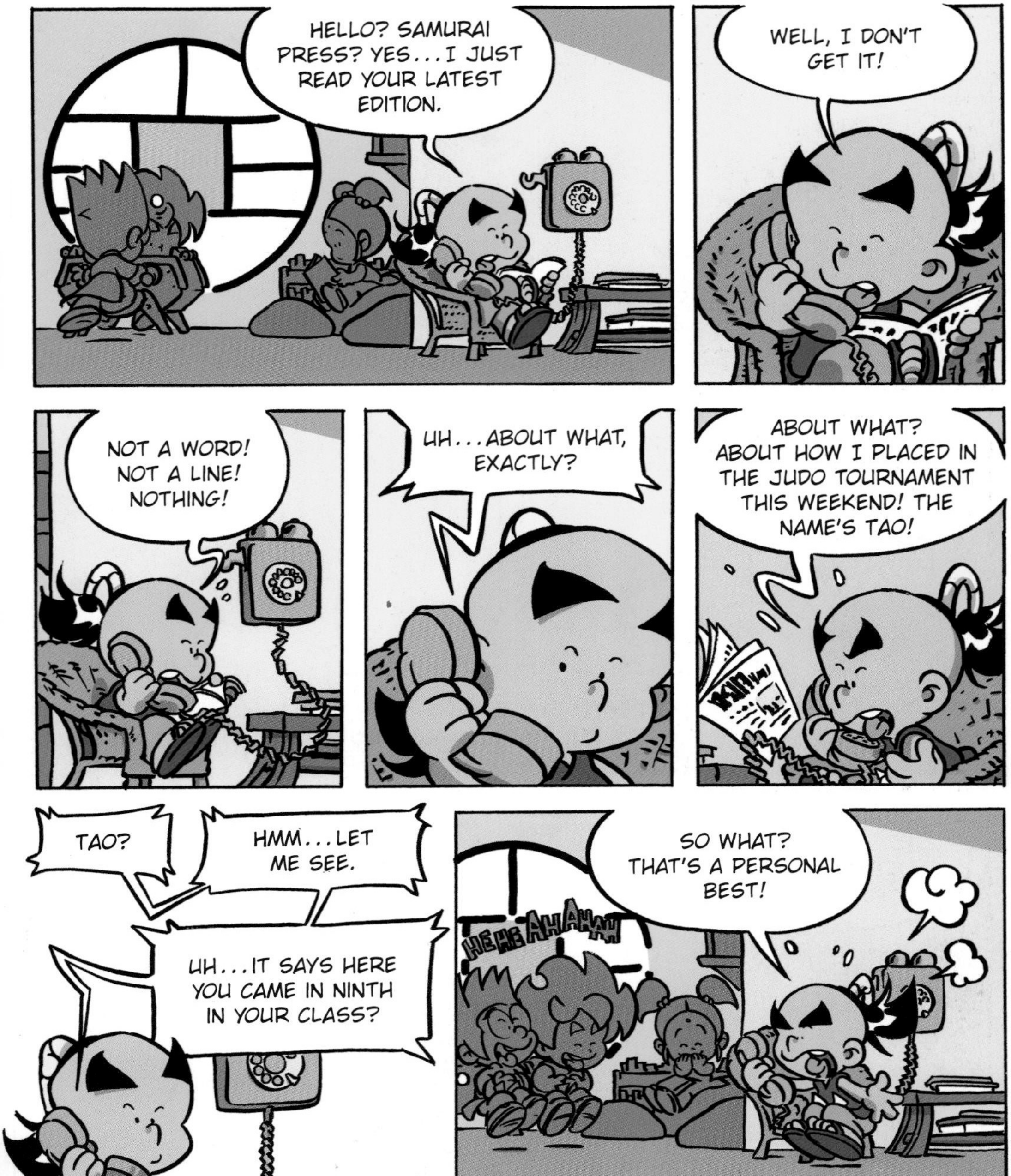
HELLO? SAMURAI PRESS? YES...I JUST READ YOUR LATEST EDITION.
WELL, I DON'T GET IT!
NOT A WORD! NOT A LINE! NOTHING!
UH...ABOUT WHAT, EXACTLY?
ABOUT WHAT? ABOUT HOW I PLACED IN THE JUDO TOURNAMENT THIS WEEKEND! THE NAME'S TAO!
TAO?
HMM...LET ME SEE.
UH...IT SAYS HERE YOU CAME IN NINTH IN YOUR CLASS?
HEHEAHAHAH
SO WHAT? THAT'S A PERSONAL BEST!

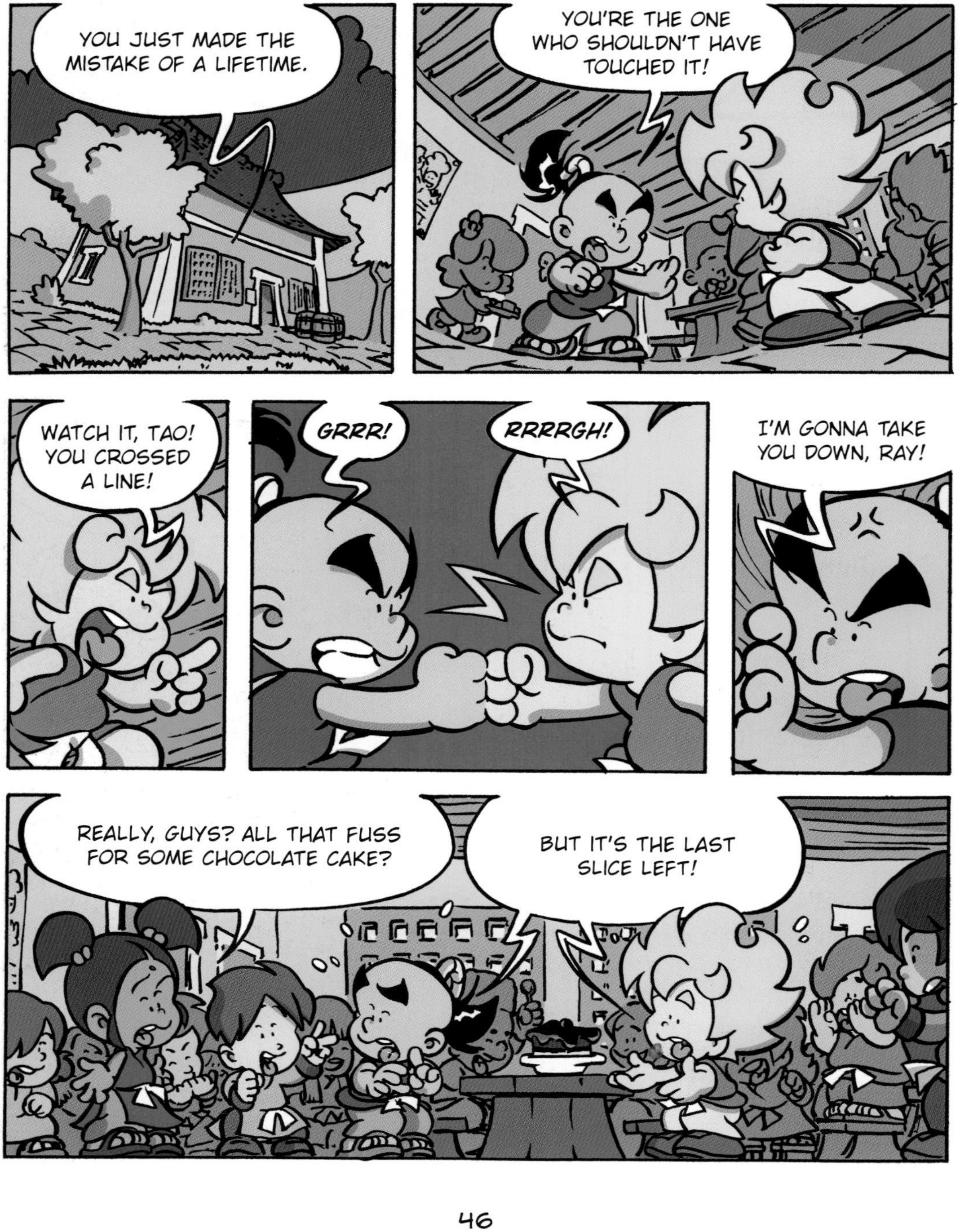

YOU JUST MADE THE MISTAKE OF A LIFETIME.
YOU'RE THE ONE WHO SHOULDN'T HAVE TOUCHED IT!
WATCH IT, TAO! YOU CROSSED A LINE!
GRRR!
RRRRGH!
I'M GONNA TAKE YOU DOWN, RAY!
REALLY, GUYS? ALL THAT FUSS FOR SOME CHOCOLATE CAKE?
BUT IT'S THE LAST SLICE LEFT!

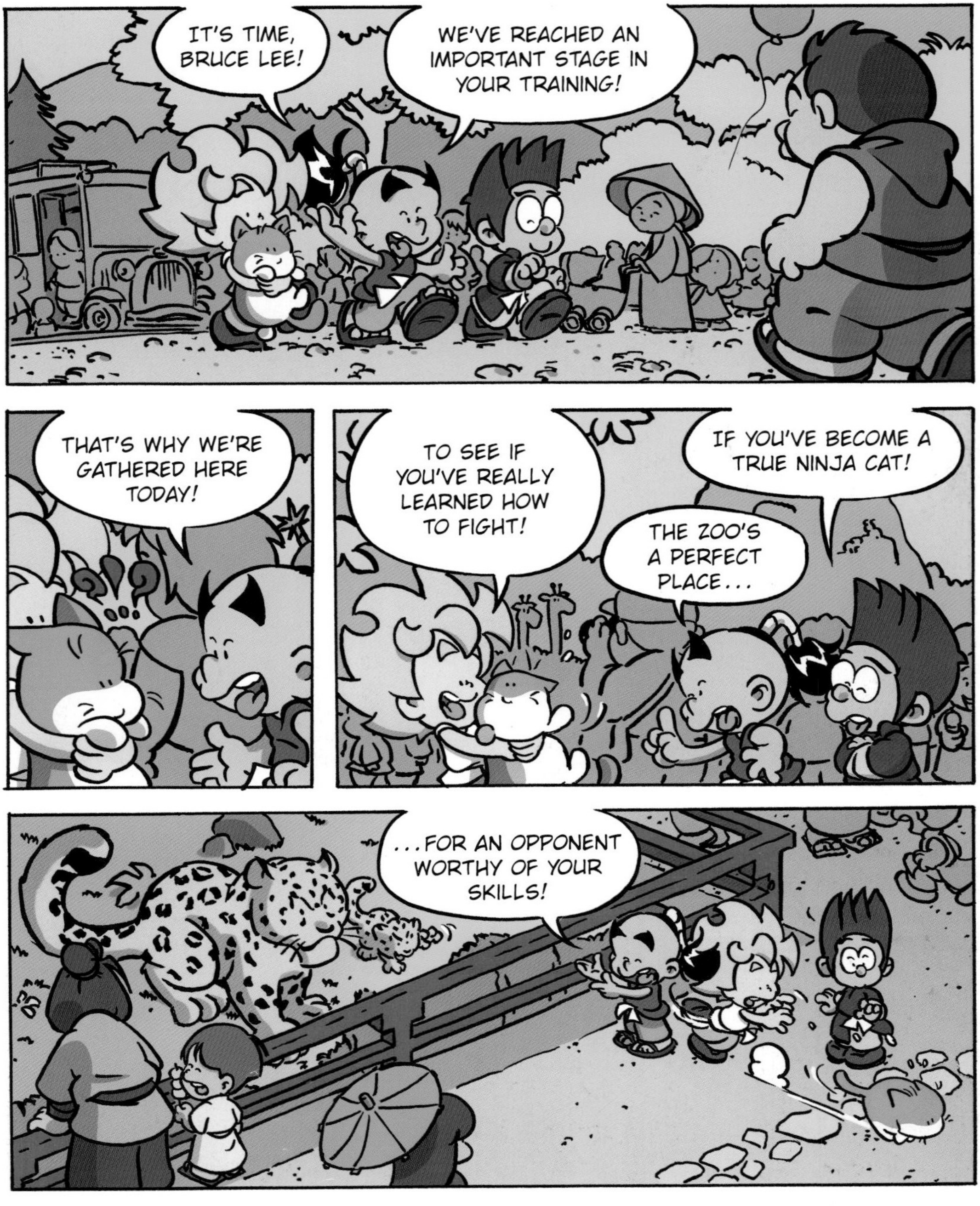
IT'S TIME, BRUCE LEE!
WE'VE REACHED AN IMPORTANT STAGE IN YOUR TRAINING!
THAT'S WHY WE'RE GATHERED HERE TODAY!
TO SEE IF YOU'VE REALLY LEARNED HOW TO FIGHT!
IF YOU'VE BECOME A TRUE NINJA CAT!
THE ZOO'S A PERFECT PLACE...
...FOR AN OPPONENT WORTHY OF YOUR SKILLS!

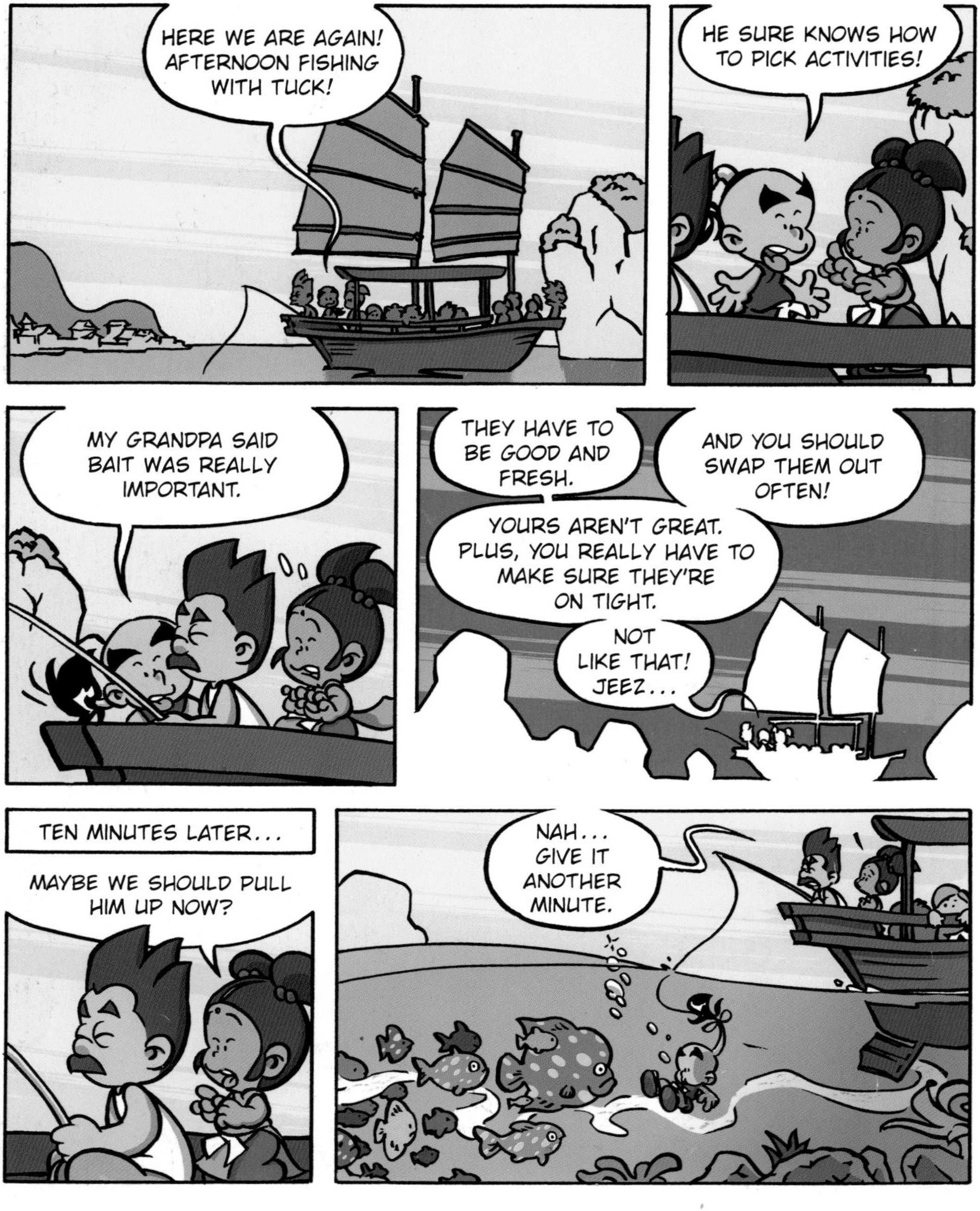
HERE WE ARE AGAIN! AFTERNOON FISHING WITH TUCK!
HE SURE KNOWS HOW TO PICK ACTIVITIES!
MY GRANDPA SAID BAIT WAS REALLY IMPORTANT.
THEY HAVE TO BE GOOD AND FRESH.
AND YOU SHOULD SWAP THEM OUT OFTEN!
YOURS AREN'T GREAT. PLUS, YOU REALLY HAVE TO MAKE SURE THEY'RE ON TIGHT.
NOT LIKE THAT! JEEZ...
TEN MINUTES LATER...
MAYBE WE SHOULD PULL HIM UP NOW?
NAH... GIVE IT ANOTHER MINUTE.

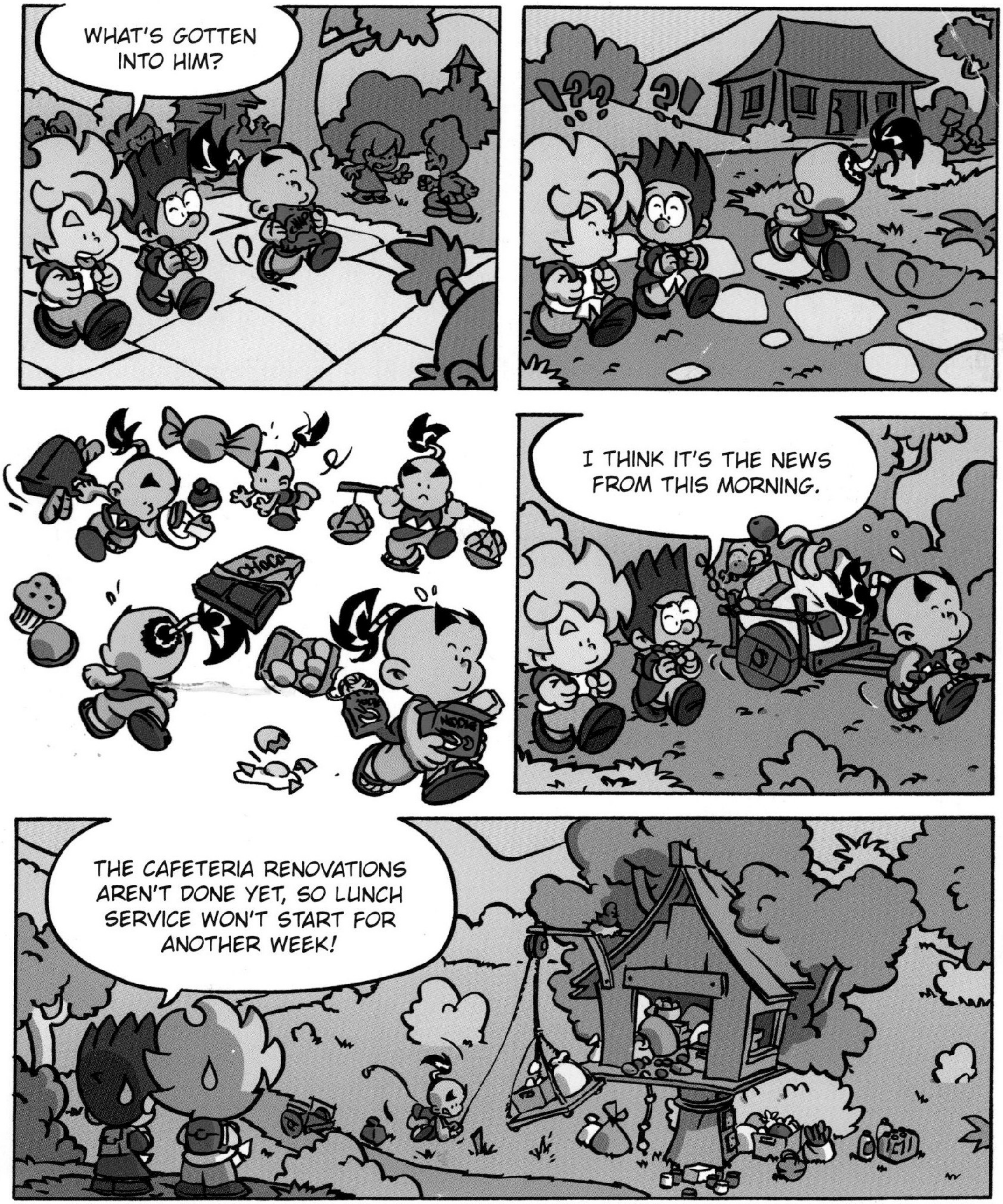
WHAT'S GOTTEN INTO HIM?
!??
?!
CHOCO
I THINK IT'S THE NEWS FROM THIS MORNING.
THE CAFETERIA RENOVATIONS AREN'T DONE YET, SO LUNCH SERVICE WON'T START FOR ANOTHER WEEK!

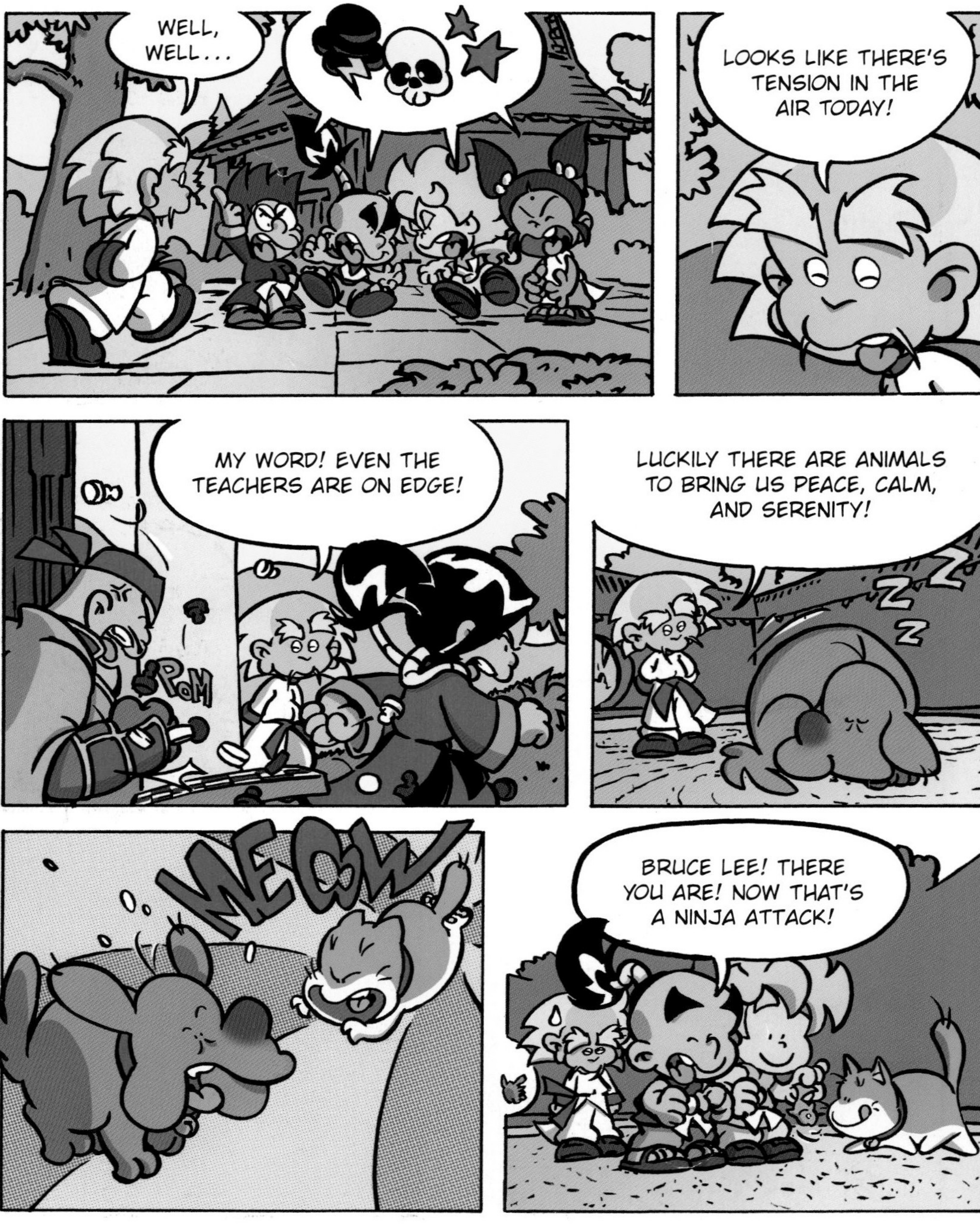
WELL, WELL...
LOOKS LIKE THERE'S TENSION IN THE AIR TODAY!
MY WORD! EVEN THE TEACHERS ARE ON EDGE!
OW
POM
LUCKILY THERE ARE ANIMALS TO BRING US PEACE, CALM, AND SERENITY!
MEOW
BRUCE LEE! THERE YOU ARE! NOW THAT'S A NINJA ATTACK!

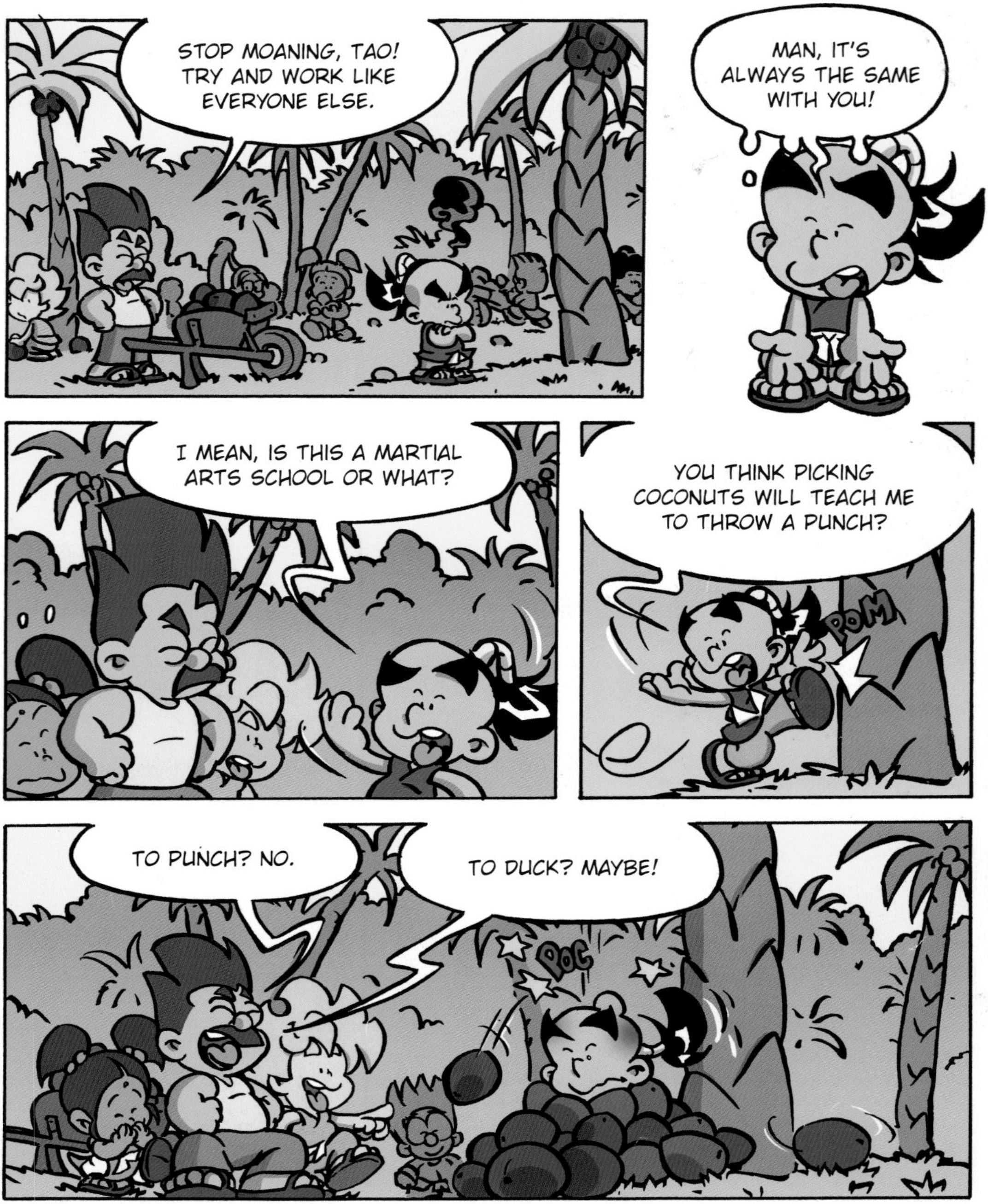
STOP MOANING, TAO! TRY AND WORK LIKE EVERYONE ELSE.
MAN, IT'S ALWAYS THE SAME WITH YOU!
I MEAN, IS THIS A MARTIAL ARTS SCHOOL OR WHAT?
YOU THINK PICKING COCONUTS WILL TEACH ME TO THROW A PUNCH?
POM
TO PUNCH? NO.
TO DUCK? MAYBE!
POC

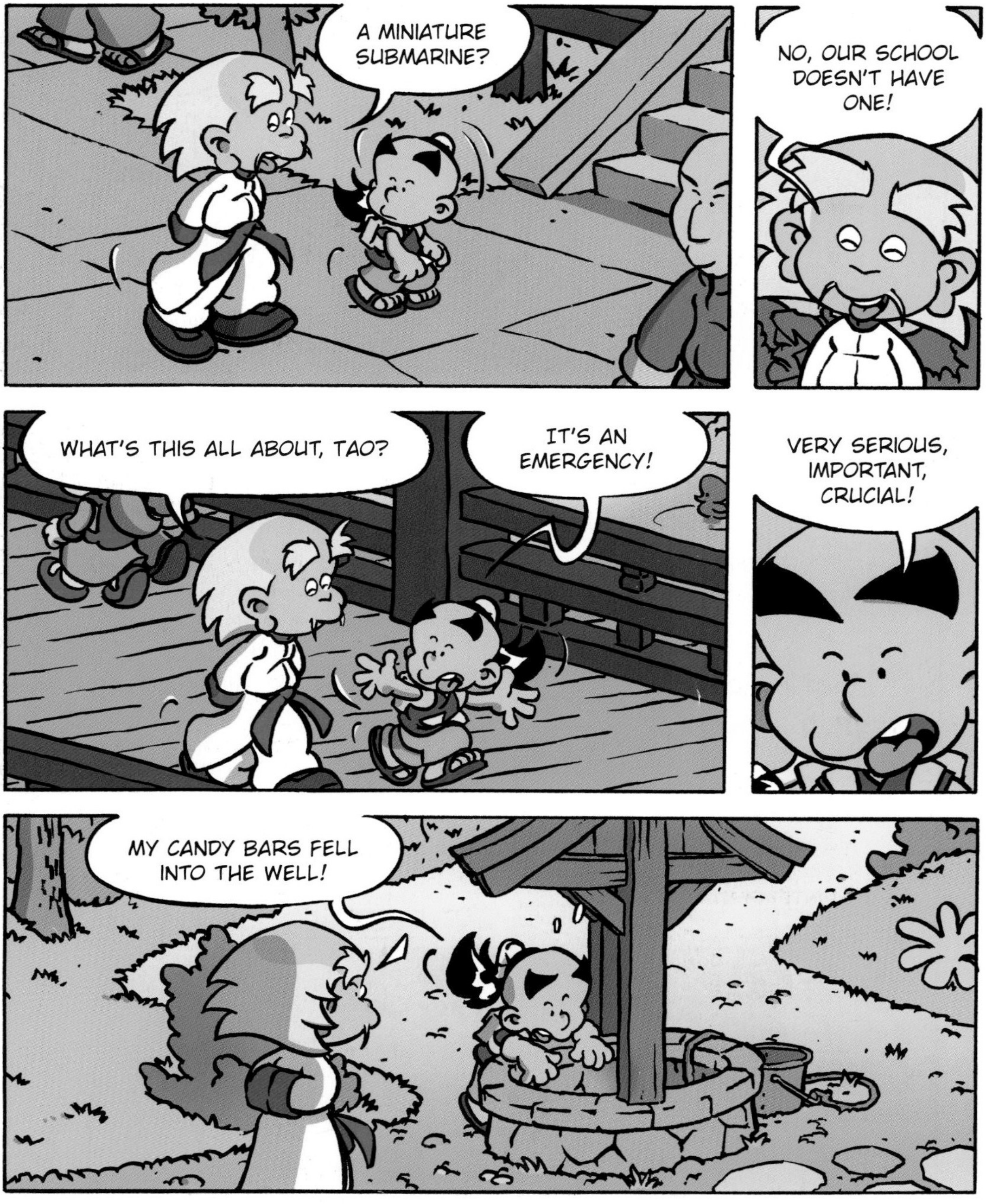
A MINIATURE SUBMARINE?
NO, OUR SCHOOL DOESN'T HAVE ONE!
WHAT'S THIS ALL ABOUT, TAO?
IT'S AN EMERGENCY!
VERY SERIOUS, IMPORTANT, CRUCIAL!
MY CANDY BARS FELL INTO THE WELL!

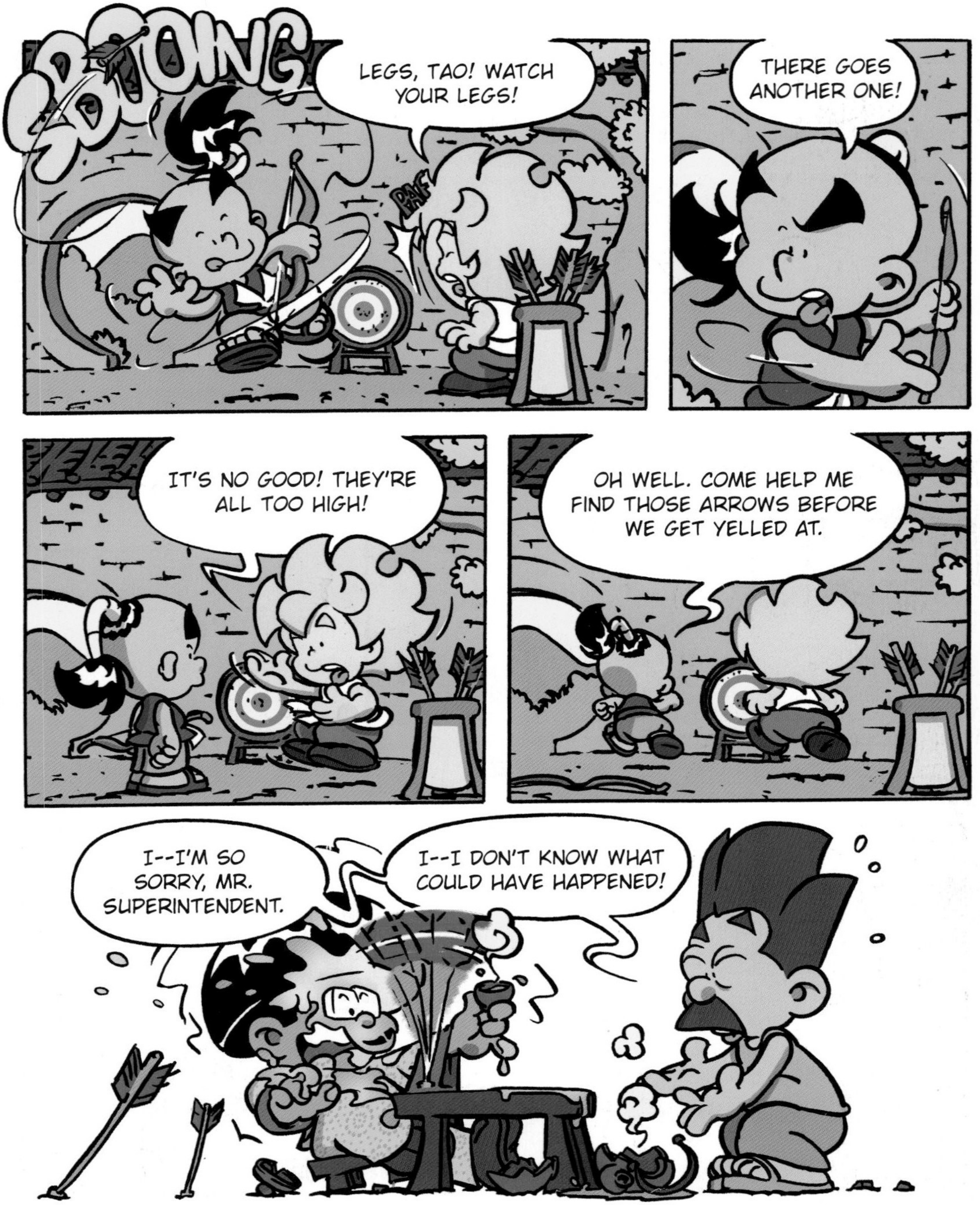
SBOING
LEGS, TAO! WATCH YOUR LEGS!
PAF
THERE GOES ANOTHER ONE!
IT'S NO GOOD! THEY'RE ALL TOO HIGH!
OH WELL. COME HELP ME FIND THOSE ARROWS BEFORE WE GET YELLED AT.
I--I'M SO SORRY, MR. SUPERINTENDENT.
I--I DON'T KNOW WHAT COULD HAVE HAPPENED!

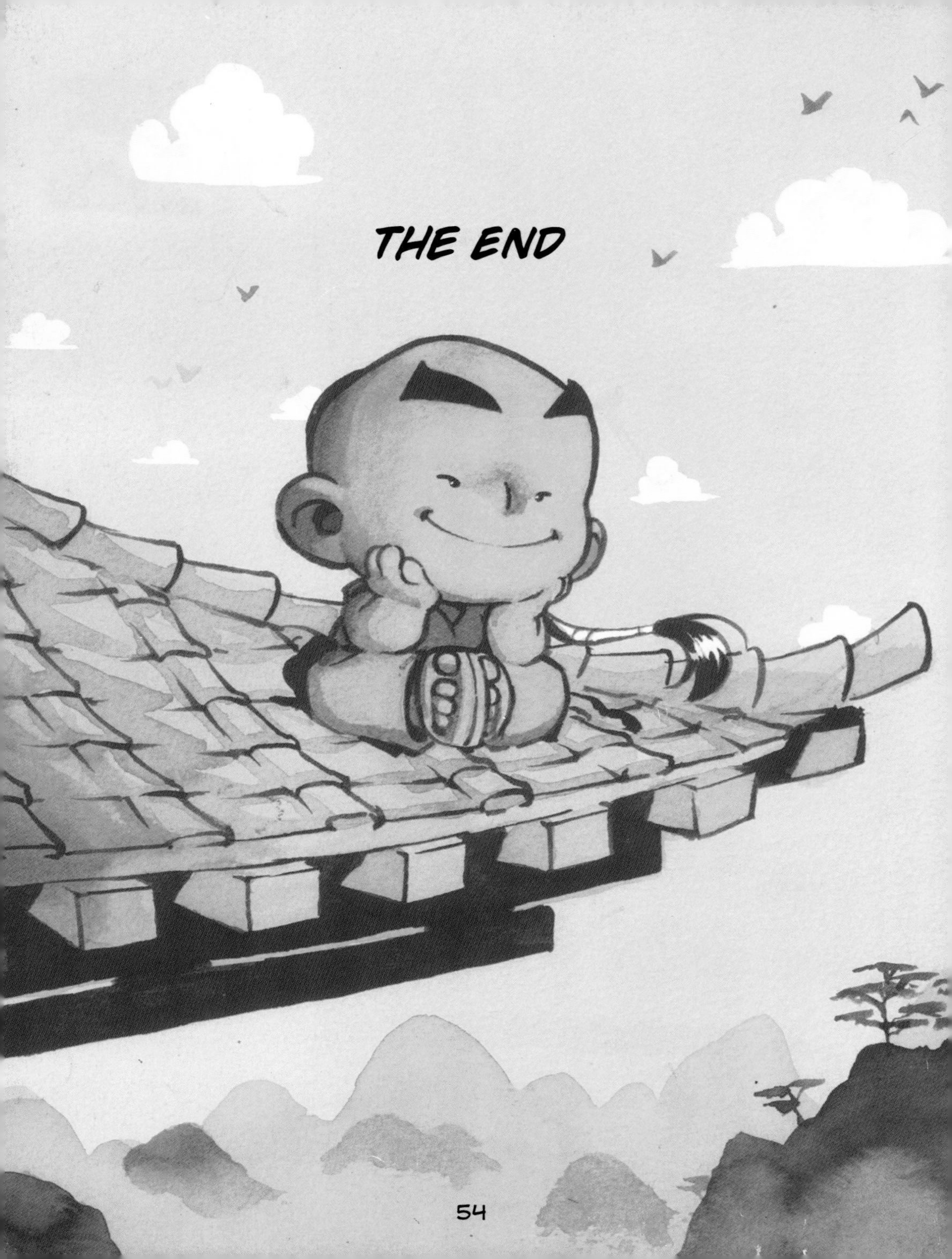
THE END

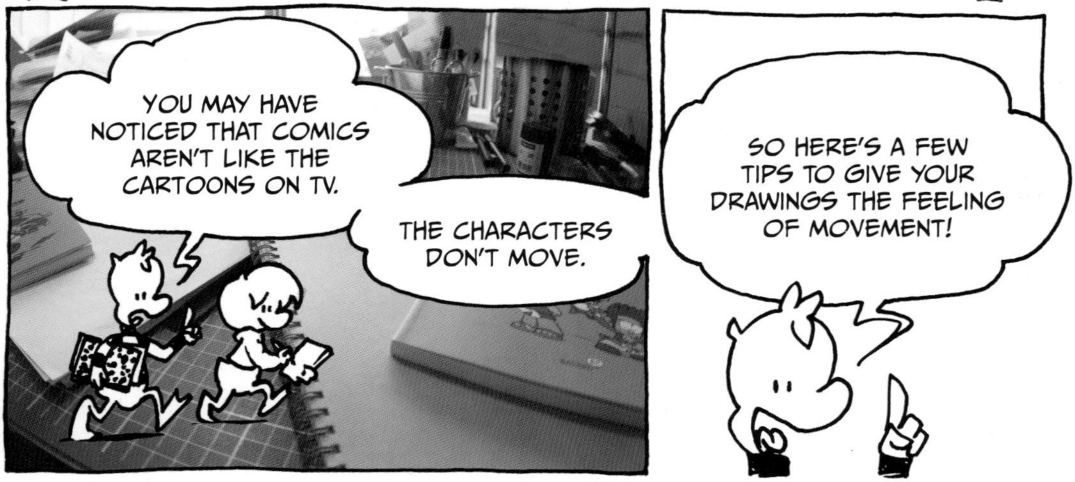
YOU MAY HAVE NOTICED THAT COMICS AREN'T LIKE THE CARTOONS ON TV.
THE CHARACTERS DON'T MOVE.
SO HERE'S A FEW TIPS TO GIVE YOUR DRAWINGS THE FEELING OF MOVEMENT!

1. Speed Lines

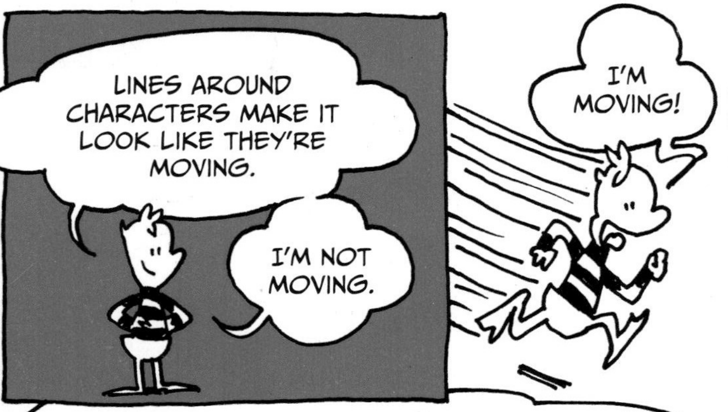
LINES AROUND CHARACTERS MAKE IT LOOK LIKE THEY'RE MOVING.
I'M NOT MOVING.
I'M MOVING!

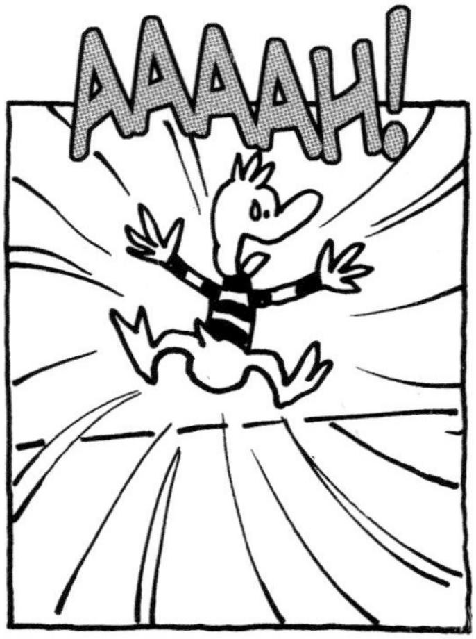
AAAAH!

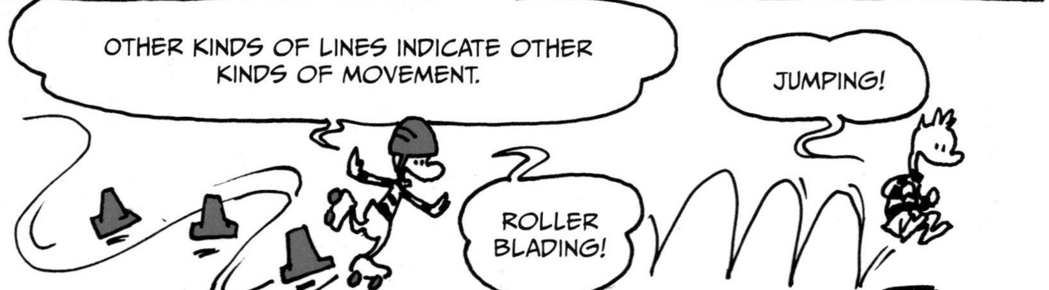
OTHER KINDS OF LINES INDICATE OTHER KINDS OF MOVEMENT.
ROLLER BLADING!
JUMPING!

2. Repetition

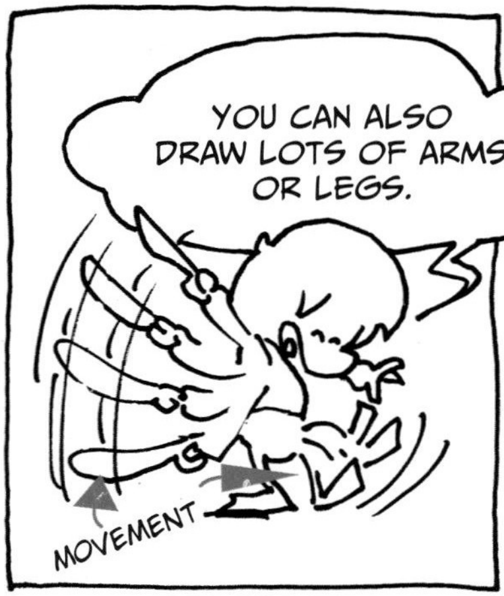
YOU CAN ALSO DRAW LOTS OF ARMS OR LEGS.
MOVEMENT

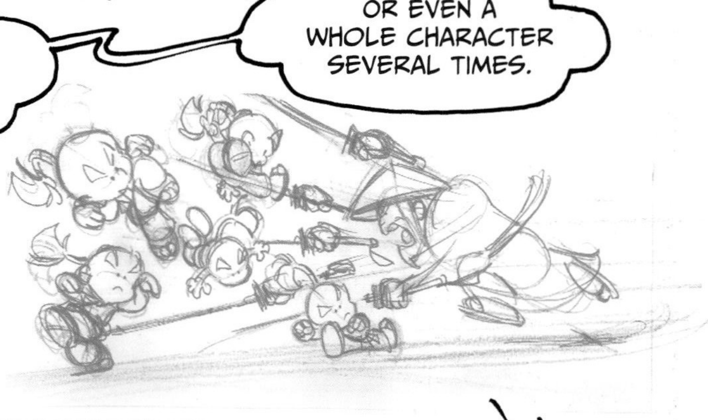
OR EVEN A WHOLE CHARACTER SEVERAL TIMES.

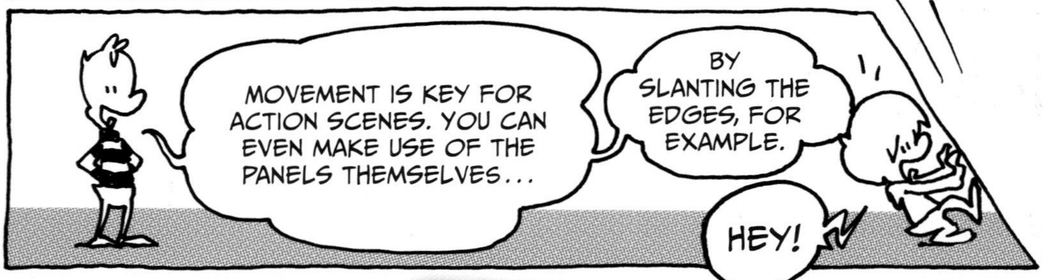
MOVEMENT IS KEY FOR ACTION SCENES. YOU CAN EVEN MAKE USE OF THE PANELS THEMSELVES...
BY SLANTING THE EDGES, FOR EXAMPLE.
HEY!

3. Layouts

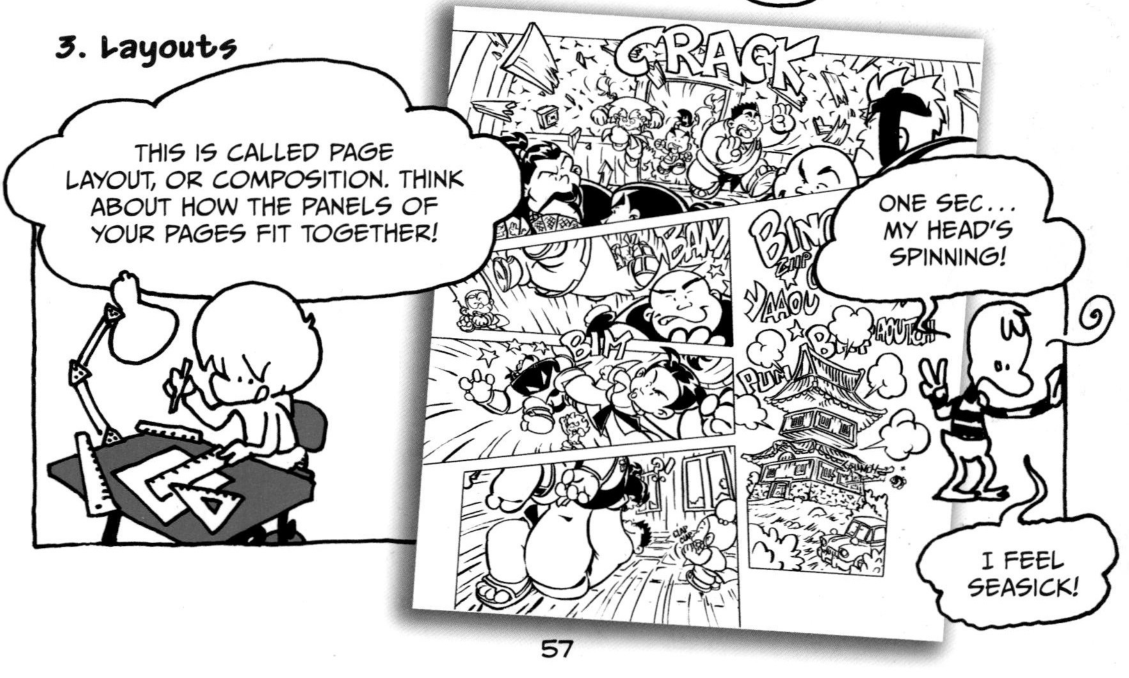
THIS IS CALLED PAGE LAYOUT, OR COMPOSITION. THINK ABOUT HOW THE PANELS OF YOUR PAGES FIT TOGETHER!
CRACK
ONE SEC... MY HEAD'S SPINNING!
I FEEL SEASICK!

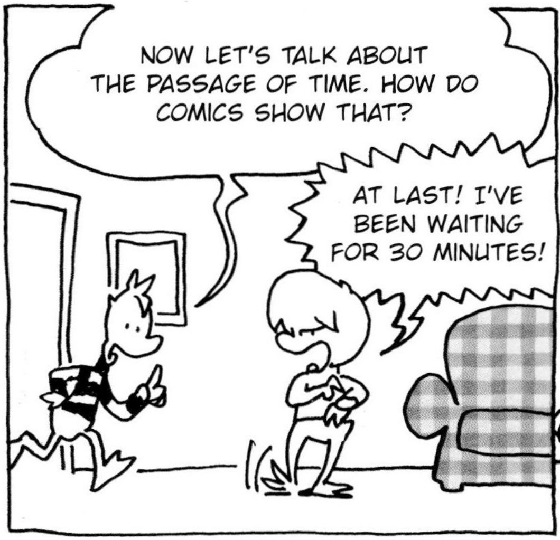
NOW LET'S TALK ABOUT THE PASSAGE OF TIME. HOW DO COMICS SHOW THAT?
AT LAST! I'VE BEEN WAITING FOR 30 MINUTES!

1. Clues

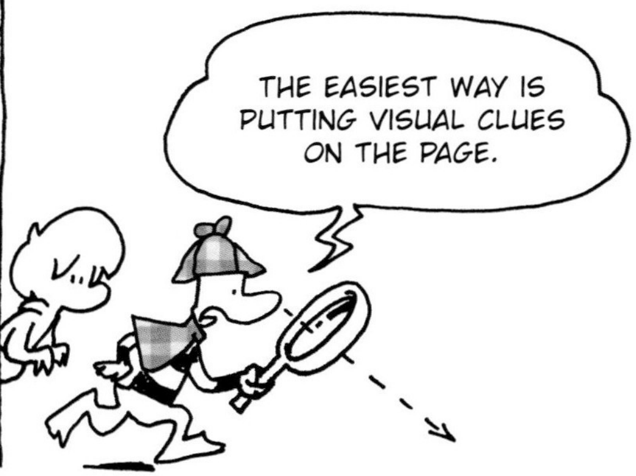
THE EASIEST WAY IS PUTTING VISUAL CLUES ON THE PAGE.

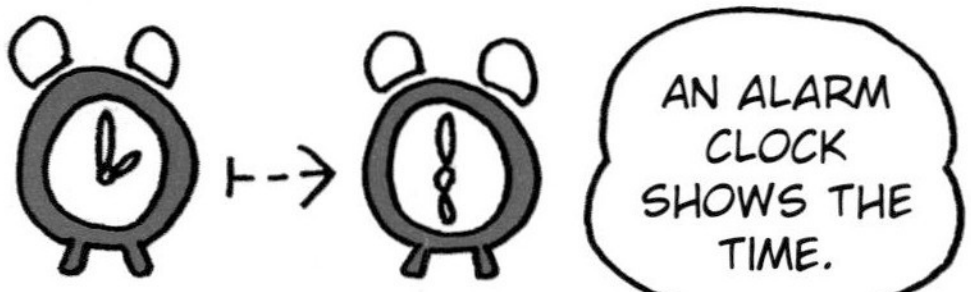
AN ALARM CLOCK SHOWS THE TIME.

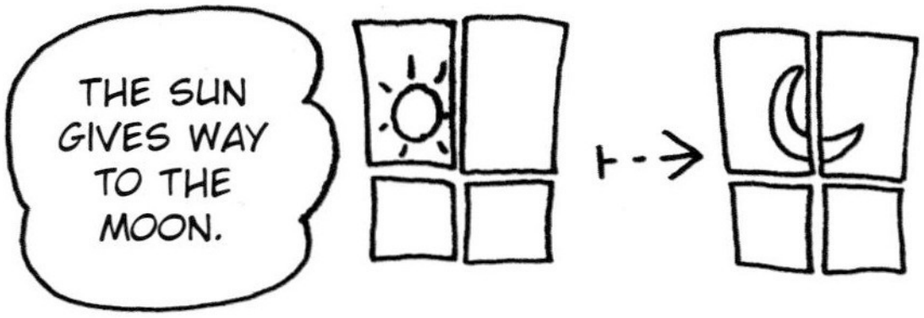
THE SUN GIVES WAY TO THE MOON.

2. Captions

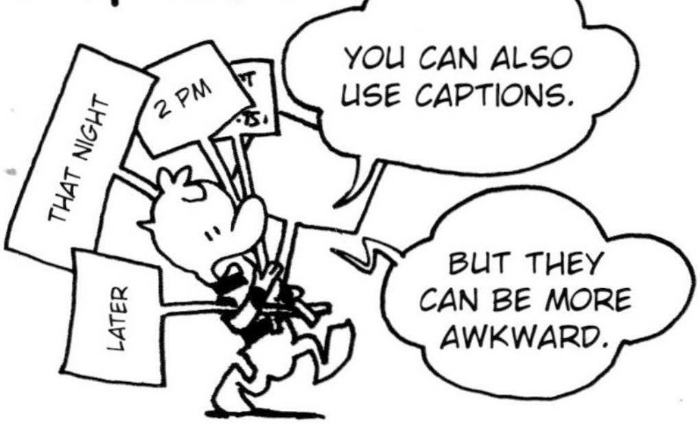
THAT NIGHT
2 PM
LATER
YOU CAN ALSO USE CAPTIONS.
BUT THEY CAN BE MORE AWKWARD.

3. Order of Panels

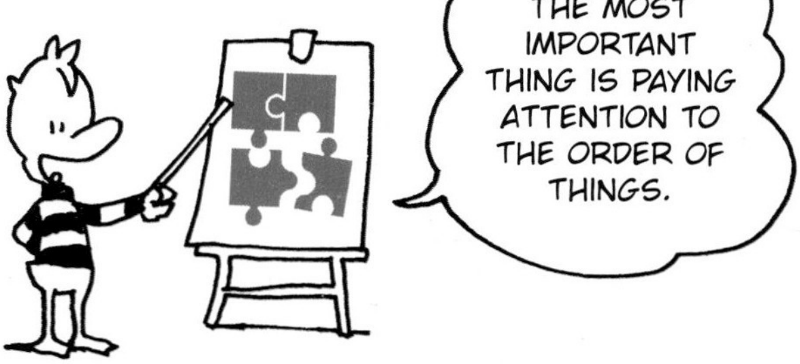
THE MOST IMPORTANT THING IS PAYING ATTENTION TO THE ORDER OF THINGS.

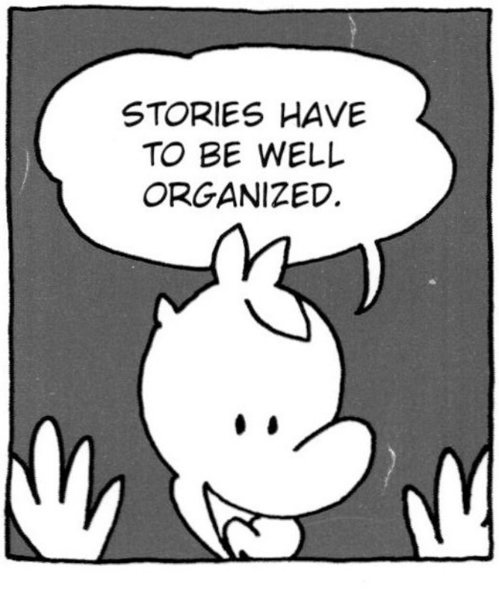
STORIES HAVE TO BE WELL ORGANIZED.

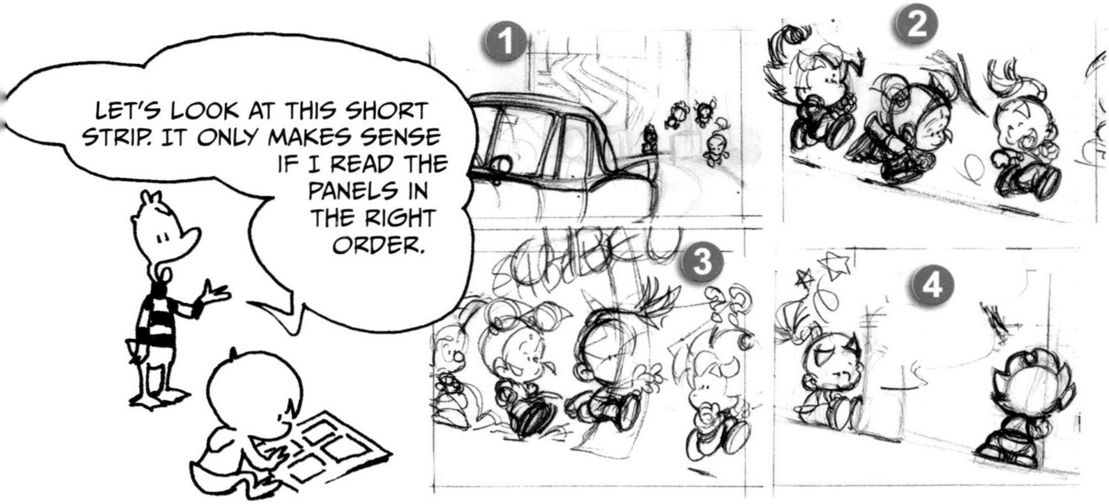
LET'S LOOK AT THIS SHORT STRIP. IT ONLY MAKES SENSE IF I READ THE PANELS IN THE RIGHT ORDER.
1
2
3
4

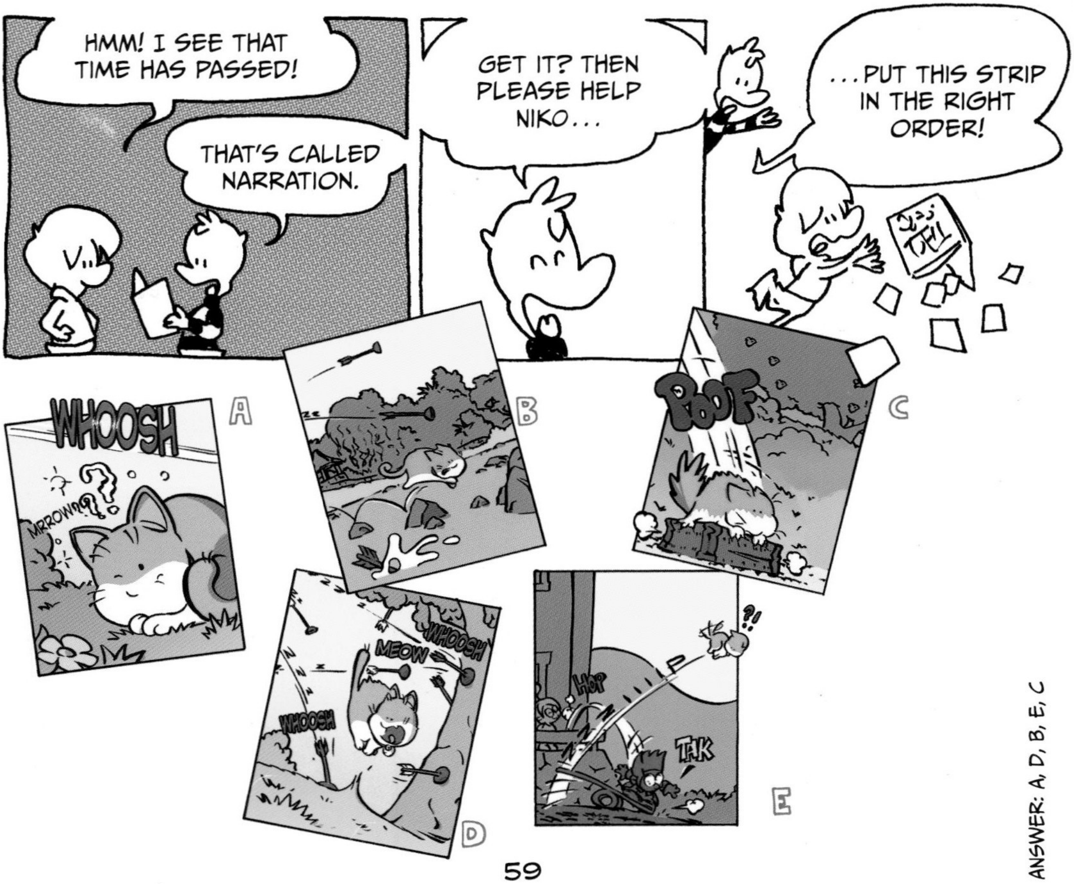
HMM! I SEE THAT TIME HAS PASSED!
THAT'S CALLED NARRATION.
GET IT? THEN PLEASE HELP NIKO...
...PUT THIS STRIP IN THE RIGHT ORDER!
WHOOSH
MRROW?
A
B
POOF
C
WHOOSH
MEOW
WHOOSH
D
HOP
?!
TAK
E

ANSWER: A, D, B, E, C

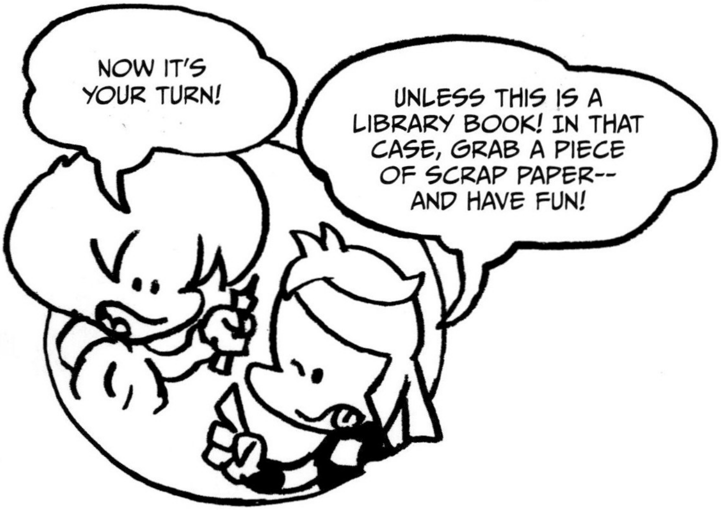
NOW IT'S YOUR TURN!
UNLESS THIS IS A LIBRARY BOOK! IN THAT CASE, GRAB A PIECE OF SCRAP PAPER-- AND HAVE FUN!

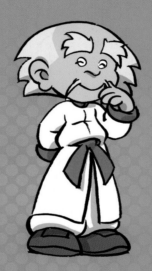

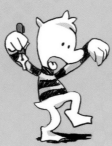

ABOUT THE AUTHOR

Laurent Richard worked in the world of advertising before becoming a professor of graphic arts. He now divides his time between teaching and illustration for children's publishing and media.

ABOUT THE ILLUSTRATOR

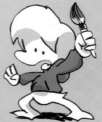

Nicolas Ryser attended the School of Graphic Arts Estienne in Paris. He won several competitions including the Angoulême and works for the magazine *Casus Belli*. He was recently awarded a *Graine de pro* ("Seed of a professional") prize.

TAO

The Little Samurai

#1 Pranks and Attacks!
#2 Ninjas and Knock Outs!
#3 Clowns and Dragons!
#4 The Championship!
#5 Wild Animals!

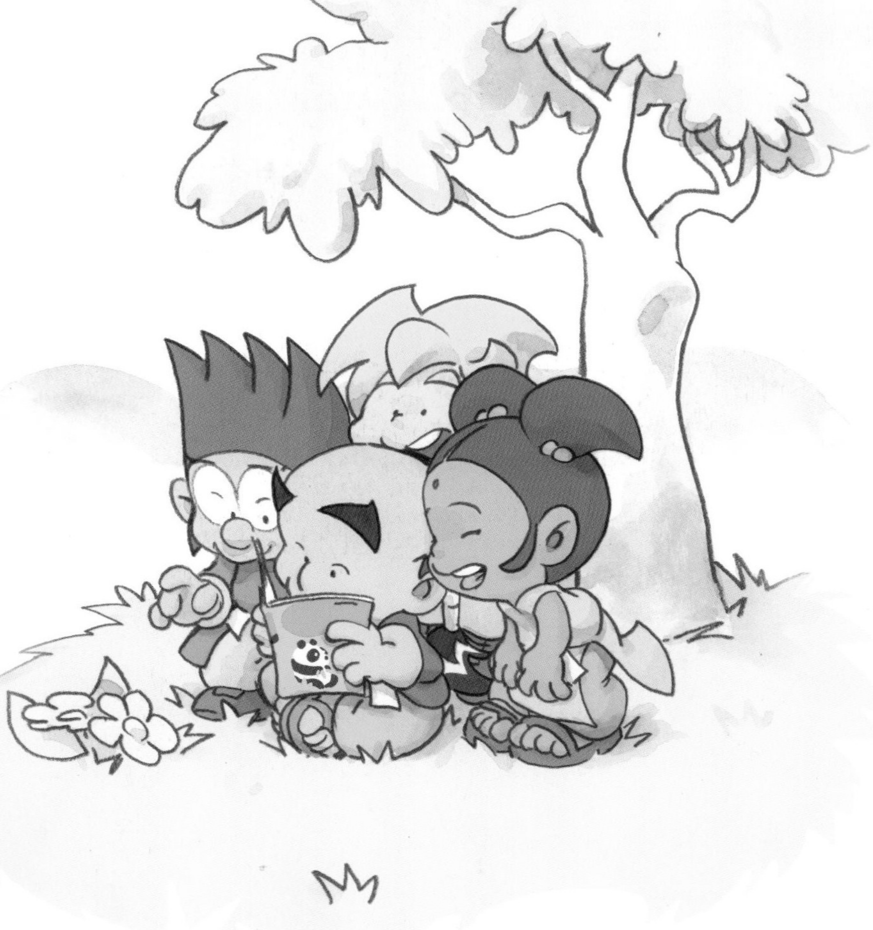

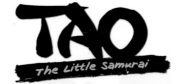

P9-DWS-805